Annie Thomas

False Colours

Vol. I

Annie Thomas

False Colours
Vol. I

ISBN/EAN: 9783337054632

Printed in Europe, USA, Canada, Australia, Japan

Cover: Foto ©Andreas Hilbeck / pixelio.de

More available books at **www.hansebooks.com**

FALSE COLOURS.

A Novel.

BY

ANNIE THOMAS,

(MRS. PENDER CUDLIP),

AUTHOR OF "SIR VICTOR'S CHOICE," "DENIS DONNE,"
ETC., ETC.

IN THREE VOLUMES.

VOL. I.

LONDON:

TINSLEY BROTHERS, 18, CATHERINE ST., STRAND.
1869.

CONTENTS.

FALSE COLOURS.

CHAPTER I.

THE VARGRAVES.

" YES, pleasant society enough ; but about as much like the real thing, the thing I mean, as those gardens are like country-house gardens, or as I am like you, Isabelle—to go even wider of a well-defined mark than I have gone before."

" Poor dear Cecile ! when will your fate and will agree ?" a second speaker said, cheerfully; " now as far as ignominious 'me' is concerned, I am quite happy in this society, that you find pleasant enough : it's as good as we can ever hope to mix in, you know that, Cecile ; and after all, who is more respected and looked up to than papa, about here ?"

" No one," the one who had spoken first, a girl of about twenty-seven, answered, quickly, laughing as readily as she spoke. " No one ;

and that proves so much, doesn't it? Proves
that the neighbourhood is so entirely right,
and he is so entirely worthy, and I am so
utterly in the wrong in not finding everything
all-sufficient. Well, how are we to mix in
'pleasant society' this day? that is all I ask."

" Why, there is Mrs. Foster's garden-party
—don't pretend to have forgotten that."

" No, I won't; and after this garden-party,
there is a long dark hour of nothingness, and
then the hour with the company of singers we
have been beguiled into joining, and then bed,
and then the consciousness of a day well spent
to soothe us to slumber."

" Cecile, how you do contrive to grate on
one's feelings!" This second speaker was a
young lady about twenty-one. " You don't
like to be quite happy yourself, and so you
won't let me be quite happy when I have
everything to make me so; where did you get
your discontent from? not from the Vargraves,
I am sure."

" Don't bother your brains by attempting to
solve the mystery of my discontent," Cecile
answered, with good-natured, tolerant scorn-

fulness; "let me have your white chip-hat, to arrange some rose-buds in for the benefit of Mrs. Foster's guests; and don't tell your father what I have been saying; don't, please, dear."

She went out of the room as she made this request, and made her way up to her own bed-room, singing blithely enough as she went. She, Cecile Vargrave, was only the niece of this house in which she lived, and the one with whom she had been talking was the only daughter. But it had always been Mr. Vargrave's aim, and Mrs. Vargrave's ambition, that neither observant friends, nor the girls themselves, should be able to detect any differ-ence in the manner of their treatment. But though the treatment had been applied for the last five years, the treated ones did not in the slightest degree resemble one another. The twigs had both been carefully bent in precisely the same direction. But the one was of stronger growth than the other. Cecile, who had it in her power to do so much, had it in her will to do so little, that Mrs. Vargrave found herself at times giving unwilling heed to the memory of the scandal she had heard of Cecile's mother

having been a woman who was strongly suspected of no origin at all. The girl had lived
with them for the last five years. She had
been taken to the same safe marts, she had
been adorned by the taste of the same milliner.
The same riding-master had instructed Isabelle
and her to come down to their saddles, and
swing off in a canter, without any other movement than a gentle swerve, however hard their
horses pulled, during the hours of fullest
excitement in the Row. Yet for all these
advantages, and a thousand others which
cannot be enumerated here, Cecile, to the best
of Mrs. Vargrave's knowledge, was as absolutely
unsought as when she had come to Bayswater,
fresh from a struggling life somewhere, five
years ago.

She came into such a different atmosphere
—an atmosphere which was redolent of peace,
and plenty, and respectability—and yet she
could never bring herself heartily to feel and
declare that the one she had left was less
pleasant to her. "How rejoiced you must be
to have nothing more to do with the humours
of landladies, and the discomforts of third-rate

lodging-houses," Mrs. Vargrave would say to her husband's niece, pityingly. "My poor child, your mother seems to have been utterly unable to combat real-life difficulties of any sort." This, Mrs. Vargrave would say after Cecile had given a vivid account of how they had been routed here by insolence, and made to flee thither by impostures. And then Cecile would return all Mrs. Vargrave's sympathy, unused, by saying:

"I rejoice in this, in your kindness, of course, aunt; but that was fun of a sort, and neither mamma nor I ever fretted about it. Quick marches and unexpected turnings out never upset us; we were vagabonds at heart, I believe."

This was a dreadful speech for a girl to make who was situated as Cecile was situated. "She does not know the full meaning o her own words, and she destroys herself," Mrs. Vargrave would say, hopelessly; "do all we can, we shall not be able to say anything of her mother that any one can care to hear, and the time will come, when Cecile marries, that we shall be asked questions."

"I can answer all I am asked with a clear conscience," Mr. Vargrave would reply to this; "I know nothing, I suspect nothing, I can say nothing."

"That is all very well and very clever, James; but it will reasonably be asked how, then, did you come to have the charge of the child?"

"I can answer even that; she arrived, with two large trunks and a shaven poodle, late one night, just as we were going to bed, if I remember rightly—announced herself as my niece, and handed me a letter from my dead brother, entrusting her to my care."

"And all this only makes it more than desirable that she should not speak of her mother, of whom we know nothing, and herself as 'vagabonds at heart,'" Mrs. Vargrave said, earnestly; "she is nearly twenty-eight now, James, and Isabelle is of age; it is time we thought seriously of their settling."

"We have been thinking seriously about it ever since Isabelle was seventeen; additional serious thoughts on this subject will wear me out; besides, I don't want to get rid of them."

"Nor do I want to get rid of them; but we can't stay with them always, and really it's of Cissy I am thinking most, if anything should happen to us; Isabelle will always win friends."

"And Cecile, if I'm not mistaken, will always command fortune. I hear them coming now. I told them to show themselves to me before they went to Mrs. Foster's garden folly." Then the two girls came into the room, and stood to be inspected. While they are being reviewed, an attempt shall be made to describe them and their home.

This latter was situated in pleasant Bayswater, in one of those wide, open roads branching out of one of the older squares, which have, amongst their chief attractions, the fact that they are close to Hyde Park and Kensington Gardens. Between this road and the highway which runs along outside the Park railings up to the Marble Arch, a long, large span of ornamental ground, called Ladbroke Square, lies, and this square was to be the scene this afternoon of the croquet-party to which the Misses Vargrave were bidden.

Mr. Vargrave had lived in this Bayswater

district from a period long anterior to its becoming the fashionably prosperous place it now
is.   He had rented a house on the same site as
the one he had since built and now occupied,
for many years, until, indeed, Fortune smiled
upon him with sufficient brightness to justify
him to himself in such expenditure.   Then he
realized one of his wife's day-dreams, and
enabled her to live in "a house of their own,"
a proceeding which she had a vague idea, whatever the original cost, must be more economical
than being obliged constantly to disburse for
rent and taxes.

It is difficult to say exactly what Mr. Vargrave
was.   He spoke of himself as an Italian ware-
houseman on a wholesale scale, but this Mrs.
Vargrave expressly desired might be considered
as merely one of Mr. Vargrave's jokes.   True,
he imported dried fruits and dry wines on an
extensive and remunerative system, but this he
did outside some even larger transactions on
the Stock Exchange, on which he must have
had some sort of agency, or with which he
must have had some safe and agreeable understanding; for he never played see-saw on an

exaggerated scale. He was not a beggar one
week, and a millionnaire the next. In fact, he
was a safe man in all respects, and one who
was well reputed (as his daughter Isabelle said)
all round the region in which they dwelt. Well-
reputed not only as one who could pay his way
promptly, however liberally his way might lead
him, but also as a sagacious, keen, intelligent
man, who was capital ballast to the light-
hearted, light-headed lady, his wife.

At the time of her introduction to the reader,
Mrs. Vargrave was a handsome, happy-looking
matron of forty. A well-satisfied wife, and a
not unreasonably proud mother, and a " very
model aunt," her husband's niece, Cecile Vargrave, declared. Two-and-twenty years ago her
husband had fallen in love with her sweet
beauty, and had married her for it, hopeful of
nothing beyond, and perfectly contented with it.
But he got more than he had bargained for
with himself. In addition to her sweet beauty
she had a sweet temper, and a heart so light
and affectionate, that he consistently forgave
and overlooked all the faults and follies of her
equally light head.

Not that these were very numerous, or that they were of much importance, now that he was wealthy and prosperous. But time was when he had been a hard-working, poor, and struggling man; and at that time, his wife's inability to make the calculation that five purchases of the value of twenty pounds each would amount to a hundred when viewed *en masse*, was very trying to him. It was not that she had a weak woman's desire to lavish money for the sake of show; but she was utterly unable to look beyond the hour and the counters whereon the things looked so pretty. It was certainly no regardlessness of, or indifference to, money that actuated her; for when the bills came in, she would bemoan herself freely and honestly, and launch out accusations of imposition in their charges against the most unexceptionable tradesmen. "It is a matter of fact that the bill is a mistake, or an imposition, James," she would say, earnestly; "why, I was only in the shop five minutes, and here's twenty pounds! Common sense tells you it is a mistake on their parts, doesn't it?" "But you pro-

bably bought something during those five
minutes," he would gently insinuate. And
then Mrs. Vargrave would knit her white brow
until the blue veins stood out in clear relief,
and after a great effort at reflection, would con-
cede that she had " got one ten-guinea dress,
and a five-guinea mantle, and several other
things that didn't, all of them, come to more
than five pounds;" which last item she would
mention in a triumphant manner, as being in
itself confirmation strong of the truth of her
conviction that " the bill couldn't possibly be
twenty pounds."

But with exception of this hair-brainedness
with respect to the after-claps bills are sure to
prove, Mrs. Vargrave was neither a weak nor a
thoughtless woman. Her fair beauty, unmoved
by any strong emotion, unchequered by any
cruel reverses, lasted long after her daughter and
her niece grew up, first to divide homage with,
and then draw it nearly entirely away from,
her. And she accepted the situation. Never
for a moment, light-hearted woman though she
was, degenerating into a frisky matron, or
suffering her demeanour for one instant to

provoke the remark that she forgot either her years, her daughter, or her dignity.

Moreover, she was, despite that natural desire which she expressed just now to see her girls settled, an admirable mistress of a house in which young girls lived.   In a set such as that in which they visited—a semi-suburban set, in which every movement was marked, and every possible thought and hope debated and commented upon—in such a set as this even, she achieved the proud triumph of keeping the two girls almost nameless.   Yet this she effected without insisting on any depressing seclusion.   They were allowed to go to balls. No girls in town were better up in the theatres, and every point, both of actors and plays. Mr. Vargrave's Sunday dinners were things of note, and not the least attraction of his table were the two pretty cousins.   They were taken to everything that was spoken about, and that everybody declared everybody else should see. They were much addicted to giving and going to those little evening parties which are so fatally conducive to flirtations of a fragile order ; but they were never suffered to lavish themselves about the squares and shaded roads of the neighbourhood for many hours during the sultry summer days. They were never, or very rarely, on view, in becoming morning dress, on a rustic seat, practising the transparent imposture of pretending to read, or to tat, and obviously waiting to be startled by a salutation from the casual acquaintance of last night's dance or concert. While they were younger, and under orders, Mrs. Vargrave implanted a haughty detestation in their minds of the habit of " holding themselves cheap." To this they superadded, when they were grown up, a delicate instinct of reserve, which caused their seldom-made appearance in the familiar and dearly-loved haunts of Bayswater girls to be a prized thing.

But this afternoon the two pretty cousins were going by invitation to play croquet in Ladbroke Square. Mrs. Foster's garden-party was given on an important occasion—the publicly announced approaching marriage of her eldest daughter, Amelia, to a Mr. Hepburn, a Somersetshire squire of large property. Amelia was to bid farewell at this *fête* to all her young friends—to bid public farewell to them, that is; for they were severally promised that they should see a good deal of her and her dresses during the few days that were to intervene between this party and the wedding.

The two Misses Vargrave were to be head bridesmaids. They were chosen to lead the procession of eight, not so much on account of the great intimacy which existed between the families, as on account of their great superiority of look and style to any of the other Bayswater belles then out. It is time to say something about these looks of theirs. Isabelle, as the daughter of the house, claims the first place, in spite of being Cecile's junior by six years.

She had a great deal of her mother's beauty, without that sweetness which has been re-marked upon. Fair beauty, of that pale, clear, satin-skinned kind that looks high-bred, and that is generally, as in Isabelle's case, found in company with a small, thin, aquiline nose. Her hair was light brown, or would have been light brown had it been permitted to repose smoothly upon her head, as nature intended it to do. As it was, it was so much crumpled

and puffed, that where it stood up in transparent
billows on either side of the parting, it looked
pale amber-colour. Beautiful eyes of the same
light brown shade as her hair, with a touch
more of gold in their brown than was on her
locks naturally, perhaps. A figure that promised well for being full and large in after-
years; that was full indeed now; shoulders
that sprang out freely, and that had not much
droop in them; and a firm, small, round,
compact waist, that did not look as if it could
be easily compressed into a still smaller
compass. Not a tall girl, but one who carried
a fair amount of dignity, from a way she had
of holding her head well up. Which erectness
might be due to hauteur, or might be due to
tight-lacing: it was extremely difficult even for
her most intimate friend to decide the point.
A decided voice, and a decided manner towards
every one in the world save her cousin Cecile,
of whom, for some reason which she herself
was utterly unable to discover, Isabelle Vargrave stood enough in dread to make her very
deprecating. Every one said that Isabelle
was " quite a Vargrave," in spite of her having

a great deal of her mother's fair beauty, for she had her father's aquiline features, decision, and self-possession. But about Cecile this could not be said; she was not quite a Vargrave, or quite an anything else about which they knew aught. She was quite herself, quite sufficiently endowed with a power of making herself look almost plain when she had been asked out to ornament a room, and was feeling herself bored, and a power of glowing into almost beauty when she pleased to do so. Bayswater often felt as it gazed upon its unbroken ranks of unmarried daughters that it would be well rid of her. Yet this feeling did not arise from any untowardness in her own conduct. She never bewitched the lovers of their daughters, she never beguiled the affections of a son. They only felt that she could do those things if she liked, and were generally conscious of being under a lion's paw, however quietly she demeaned herself.

And the girl with the dubious antecedents and the mother about whom nothing was known, did demean herself very quietly during the trying period of her admired girlhood. Still it was hard to believe that quiet and herself had been friends from the birth. A graceful creature, full as a tigress of subtle movement, with a fervent, full, earnest-eyed face, the colouring of which was creamy and peculiar, looking dark by daylight, and very fair by night. Eyes with black pupils, and black lashes and brows, and very brown hair. A full mouth and a firm chin, and a voice that could be like a ringing bell, but that she could also tone down into something most wonderfully full and soft. Above all, with such a habit of quiet about her.

CHAPTER II.

MAY AND DECEMBER.

AMELIA FOSTER, the eldest of a family of nine, was generally allowed to have done a good thing for herself in having won the heart and the offer of the hand of Mr. Hepburn. "It is true there is a disparity as far as age is concerned, but then Amelia was always sedate beyond her years." This is what was said by the Foster family, and by friends of the Foster family; and the saying had all the strength of truth. No one could contradict or even doubt either statement. There was a slight disparity in the ages of the contracting couple, seeing that Mr. Hepburn was something over sixty, and Amelia was not twenty-one; and Amelia had always been remarkable for a certain prudence and reserve, and sedateness of bearing, which had caused her to be denominated both sly and stuck-up by her youthful compeers. But now that this cautious and discreet May was going to marry such an unmistakeable December, no one could deem her characteristics to be other than the best for her to be possessed of. Amelia had met and conquered him in the course of a visit she had paid to a friend in Paris, some short time before the period at which these chronicles commence. The engagement had been formally entered upon and announced, but Mr. Hepburn had not yet been exhibited in Bayswater. It was understood that the re-organization of Glene, his place in the country, would entirely absorb him until the wedding, and as this absorption betokened great care for the decent ordering of the establishment, and consequently great consideration for her future comforts, the bride-elect bore his absence with the most exemplary patience.

On her return from that highly successful trip to Paris in the character of a bride-elect, Amelia had deported herself with her usual admirable decorum, and had withdrawn herself

entirely from the frivolities and gaieties of the
Bayswater world. This croquet-party was the
first lapse into anything like social communion
with her old friends and school-fellows which
she had yet made, and it was to be the last
before her marriage. This concession, which
to some young girls would have partaken of the
nature of a sacrifice, was made to circumstances which many people would have re-
gretted. But Mrs. Foster, on behalf of her
daughter and the family generally, refused to
consider that there was anything to regret,
either in the age or absence of Mr. Hepburn,
the owner of Glene.

It was to be a very grand wedding ; and was
to take place the following week—the last week
in June—and Isabelle and Cecile Vargrave
were to officiate as bridesmaids on the occasion. Naturally it formed the subject of the
whole conversation between the three friends,
indeed between Amelia and every one to whom
she talked at all this day. People who knew
Miss Foster well remarked that beneath all her
customary quiet and composure, there was a
strong feeling of elation. Every allusion which

she suffered herself to make to her future state was a proud and well-satisfied one. She struck the key-note of the tune to which she meant her married life to run in the minds of that Bayswater coterie which she was about to quit, in the reply she made to an old lady who ventured to hope that she " had well considered the responsibilities which she was going to assume." " Mr. Hepburn thinks me fit for the position of the greatest importance in the county," she said, rather pompously. " People who know nothing of Glene can form no idea of what my responsibilities will be." The two Vargraves stood by and heard her say this, and mentally resolved that the gorgeous invitation she had extended to them to visit her at Glene should never be practically accepted.

Though Miss Foster literally stood in the relation of May to the December of her future husband, she was not such a fresh and glee-some embodiment of the month as to force a feeling of gentle pity from all such as beheld her. A young woman with a tall, erect, thin figure, and a handsome-featured, sharp-expressioned face, she was one who could adorn herself in the most matronly of robes, and wear it as if it was hers by right of time, if such were Mr. Hepburn's desires. She had been the eldest daughter of a house where a great deal of domestic forethought and discretion was demanded from the eldest daughter. And co-existent with this demand, and strengthening the qualities it cultivated in her, there had always lived an intense desire to free herself from its tedious claims by changing and bettering her condition.

So in furtherance of this desire Amelia Foster had never wasted her time in the ordinary frivolities of her caste and her age. She had never suffered herself to fall in love, and to her credit be it said, she had never suffered herself to flirt, or to be flirted with. She had passed a stony, unemotional girlhood, and now she had won her reward in gaining the consideration of a man who wanted a young wife, but who did not want to be worried and made jealous either of the past, the present, or the future, in his declining years. Amelia had set his mind completely at rest on the subject of his being the one lord of her allegiance during their first confidential conversation. "It is never pleasant to speak of what may take place after one's death," she had said, steadily, "still I think it may be satisfactory to you to know that I shall be quite as well pleased if you make my enjoyment of whatever you may leave me, dependent on my not marrying again, as if you leave me unfettered."

"Unsolicited, I should never have thought of binding you in such a way," Mr. Hepburn replied; "but as you wish it, I will strengthen the assurance I shall be happy to take with me into another world, that you will never bear another name than mine."

When Amelia narrated this conversation to her parents, they rather reproved her for what they deemed the injudiciousness of a request founded upon the first flash of a romantic attachment to the man she was about to marry. But Amelia quickly undeceived them.

"I care for money and position more than for anything else in the world," she said, decidedly; "I know what I am about: my offer of giving up what I never should care to have, and may never have the chance of, whether I care for it or not, has improved my prospects. Mr. Hepburn may live till I am too old to love any one else or to be loved by any one else; but I shall never be too old to enjoy luxury."

The out-door *réunion* was nearly at an end, when there came in haste from the Fosters' house, which opened into the square, two or three messengers, bearing tidings of import- ance, apparently. Mrs. Foster was addressed first, and as soon as she had listened to the address, she advanced upon her daughter. "Amelia," she said, in some anxiety, arrest- ing that tall young lady in the act of bending to circumstances, and looking for a lost ball under the sweeping branches of a laurel, "Amelia, Mr. Hepburn has arrived."

In a moment there rushed into Amelia's mind the remembrance that Mr. Hepburn was not legally her own yet, and that she had pro- mised him that she would not indulge in any more suburban dissipation between the period of his parting with her in Paris and his com- ing to claim her as his bride. For a moment she was taken by surprise, and that not a pleasant surprise, so palpably that Cecile Vargrave said—

" How fortunate that we were all on the point of going away ; come, Amelia, we shall excuse you, and Mrs. Foster will receive our adieux and disperse us ; we were all just going, we were, indeed."

" I would almost rather that Isabelle and you come in with me," Amelia said, slowly recovering herself; "you see to the rest, mamma; I must go."

" Alone, too," Cecile said, quietly.

" No, not alone ; you will see Mr. Hepburn sooner or later, and it's just as well now ; come in with me." Then the two went in together to meet a man who was to exercise such an influence over their lives as should be felt by both of them until their lives ended.

" I was out in the square with my friend, Miss Vargrave, and I have brought her in to introduce you to her," Amelia said, introducing Cecile to a tall, stout, old gentleman, who advanced to meet them as they entered the room. He was a portly, fine, upright old man of sixty-

four or five, with grey hair and a grizzled
moustache. His features were fine, unthick-
ened and unflattened by age. His complexion
was soft, fair, and delicately rosy, more like
that of a young girl than a man, old or young.
This, and the soft oiliness of a well-modulated
tone, gave him the touch of effeminacy which
struck those who saw him as being in direct
opposition to his robust and manly growth.

He was an excessively agreeable, gentlemanly man. Cecile felt the sure conviction at
first sight of him, that the judgment which
stands at the head of this paragraph had been
pronounced upon him a thousand times by any
number of old and easily pleased people. He
was a man who very much desired to be agreeable, and who furthered that desire not by any
studying of and consideration for the idiosyn-
cracies of others, but by a generous display of
his own habits, and an equally lavish display
of expectation of these habits being admired
and approved of. His bright, keen blue eyes
roved inquiringly over the faces of those on
whom he was bringing his agreeable manners
to bear, roved inquiringly and suspiciously, as

if it had occurred even to him as being within
the bounds of possibility that the recipient of
his civilities might not rank them highly as he
himself did. "A strange mixture of blandness
and volubility," Cecile thought, returning his
elaborate bow; "what a mercy that he isn't
going to bring those characteristics to bear on
a sensitive woman."

"Some of the arrangements I am making
compelled me to come to town," Mr. Hepburn
explained: "the opportunity of seeing you was
not to be missed, and I was anxious to make
my friend Mr. Scorrier known to you, Amelia."

As he spoke he turned slightly round, still
holding the hand of the lady he was going to
marry; and the two girls became conscious
that somewhere in the shade of the curtains
another gentleman was standing waiting to be
spoken to.

"I am very happy to see any friend of
yours, Mr. Hepburn," Amelia said, very properly; "papa and mamma will be very happy,
too," she added, quietly; and then she shook
hands with Mr. Scorrier, and wondered if he
had a place near Glene, and whether he ranked

as highly, or more highly, in the county than
Mr. Hepburn. Before she could take any steps
towards satisfying herself on this point, her
mother came in from a highly-successful last
view of the garden guests, and soon Mr. Foster
arrived from the City, and the future son-in-
law suffered himself to be persuaded to stay to
dinner.

Meanwhile Mr. Scorrier and Miss Vargrave
exchanged a few remarks.

" Town is very pleasant just now," he said.

"Yes, I believe it is," she replied; "the *Morning Post* and the *Court Journal* both say it is."

" But you don't quite agree with the *Morning Post* and the *Court Journal* ?"

" Yes, I do, whenever I get into their atmosphere; but, as a rule, I think there is more
dust and heat in mine than they suffer from."

" Miss Vargrave's taste inclines towards the
country," Mr. Hepburn suggested, with the
most winning smile of which he was master.

" To what is pleasant in it," Cecile said,
getting up to go away—a movement which
brought relief to the mind of her friend Miss
Foster, who was not at all well inclined that

one of her familiars should make disclosures regarding the sort of life she (Amelia) had hitherto led.

" Miss Vargrave finds everything, even change, monotonous," Amelia said, addressing both the gentlemen, when Cecile had left them; and Mr. Scorrier laughed, and said he could understand that, when the change was from trying to cure typhus to trying to mend broken legs, as it was in his case.

" My friend Mr. Scorrier has lately set up in medical practice very near to Glene," Mr. Hepburn explained, in answer to Amelia's questioning glance; " and his profession has not quite torn away all the interest he used to feel in his Paris and London life yet—it will in time."

" Of course it will in time," Mr. Scorrier laughed, with a little dash of vexation in the laugh; " about the same time, I should say, as Miss Vargrave learns to like dusty heat in London, and a career of cabbages and cows in the country."

" Reasonably-regulated minds conform to circumstances, and enable their possessors to

be happy anywhere," Amelia said, more severely than she would have spoken if Mr. Scorrier had been the scion of a powerful house
among the squirearchy, which she had at first
taken him for, instead of the mere country
surgeon he proved to be. And Mr. Scorrier
regarded the fair speaker with non-admiring
eyes. " She's a handsome, under-bred, snob
of a woman," he thought, as it fell to him to
lead her into the dining-room; " and when
she's mistress of Glene, he won't be master ;
and I shall not be welcome there ; " and as he
conjured up this possibility, Mr. Scorrier disliked the practice near Glene, upon which he
had but just entered, more heartily than ever.

In spite of the shadow of dissatisfaction
which was hanging over his face now, it could
be seen, as he took his place at the table, in the
glare of the gas, that he was a very fine, open-
faced young man. There was quite enough
easy grace in his bearing, quite enough good-
tempered arrogance in the untainted-by-pro-
vincialism tone of his voice, quite enough
assured appreciation (apparently) of his own
position in his manner, to have justified

Amelia Foster in the mistake she had made about his status at first. But he was only a country surgeon : and he came as a sample of the friends and associates of the master of Glene, of whom she had given her family and friends the impression that he only mixed with the mighty ones of the earth. She felt very much disgusted with her future lord and master, and she dared not show such disgust yet. In the midst of her anger, it occurred to her as being within the bounds of possibility that Mr. Hepburn might resent her having an eye to aught but his worthy merits.

The future bridegroom and his incongruous friend left the Fosters soon after dinner. But before he left, Mr. Hepburn further aggrieved his Amelia. " I hope it is not to be a show-wedding ? " he said.

" I have left all the arrangements to mamma."

" Then I hope you have given her to understand that I dislike unnecessary parade."

" I am afraid," Amelia said, struggling hard to subdue her rising wrath, and succeeding through the strength of the interest she had in achieving the position he could give her; "I am afraid I have thought more of the real importance of the step we shall both take that day, than of what will be going on about us; can you be angry with me?"

She asked this very softly, and she was so young and fresh in comparison with himself, that he could only assure her that anger was a feeling he should always find it impossible to indulge in towards her. "Still," he added, "as the importance of the step was your principal consideration, you might have expressed a wish against there being any unnecessary parade."

"We thought of your friends, too," she said, softly; and then he made self-command a very hard task by telling her there would only be two of his friends present, the rector of the parish in which Glene was situated, and Mr. Scorrier.

"What a fortunate thing for a young man in his position to have secured your patronage," she said, speaking very steadily and unimpressively, and so betraying unconsciously the annoyance she felt.

" Not patronage in the ordinary sense of the word. I would have you to understand that now beforehand ; it is real friendship which I feel for this young man."

" Still I can but think him very fortunate to have gained such friendship, especially in his position," the young lady said, as sweetly as she could.

" I hope he may never find that his position holds him down. I had thought it an honourable one while he fills it honourably, as I hope and trust he will, for I am interested in him as the son of an old friend."

" Indeed !" Amelia said ; " was his father a surgeon before him ?"

" His father was a—well, a long and painful story hangs to it. His father was very much to blame in early youth ; this boy has never known any parent but a mother ; you must be very kind to him, Amelia, for the sake of my old friend, who wronged both him and his mother."

Meantime the task of entertaining the subject of this conversation had devolved upon Mrs. Foster, and Mrs. Foster had essayed to do it readily enough. Her first theme was her daughter. Her second, judiciously indicated to her by Mr. Scorrier, was the Miss Vargrave whom he had seen in company with her daughter that evening.

"Miss Vargrave is a great friend of Miss Foster's, I think I understood?"

"Yes; Amelia is very fond of her; very fond, indeed; though, of course, there is a great difference in their ages."

"I should not have thought that," the guest said, politely, in the belief that Amelia had all the advantages of seniority.

"Would you not, indeed! Well, though Cecile Vargrave wears wonderfully, still I see her going fast—fast; and I grieve over it, for, as I say, what has she but her looks, poor penniless girl?" And Mrs. Foster looked depressed as she propounded this problem to the young man, who was giving signs of a dawning admiration for Cecile.

"Oh! her face is her fortune, is it?" he said, lightly.

"Yes; and I hope it may prove a fortune

to her. Amelia has insisted on her being the
first bridesmaid at her wedding."

"Will that distinction benefit Miss Vargrave
very much?" he asked, laughing.

"It will show the estimation in which we
hold her; and that, little as it is, we are glad
to do, not only for her sake, but for her
uncle's. He is most kind and generous to
her; but he is not a rich man, and he has a
daughter of his own; so if we can aid Cecile
in getting off, we will. Now, Mr. Scorrier,
don't you know any one in want of a most
excellent wife?"

"No, I don't," he said, briefly, with difficulty repressing an expression of strong disgust, as he thought, "so vulgar-minded women
blur the fair ideal many a man has of a girl.
What has that poor girl done to be degraded
by being brought to market by this old lady?
Anyway, I am glad she is to be first bridesmaid, for I shall like to see her again."

While he was so thinking, they were rejoined
by Mr. Hepburn and Amelia. In the course
of his farewell speech to his future mother-in-
law, Mr. Hepburn gave that lady to understand

that only two of his friends would grace the ceremony, one of whom was Mr. Scorrier, and that he was averse to all parade.

"But that's all nonsense, now that the dresses and breakfast are ordered," Amelia said, scornfully, when he was gone.

CHAPTER III.

GLENE.

BACK in the days of Queen Elizabeth there had been a Glene, and a Hepburn had been in possession of it. It had been but a small tenement, with towers at either end of it, in the earlier days of her Majesty's undefiled career. But a little later on, Hepburn went to Court, and deported himself so satisfactorily there, that the queen organized a progress which should take in the possibility of resting her royal person for a night or two at Glene.

In those days things were not said and done with the apparently magical velocity of to-day. The queen made her progress eventually, but a sufficiently long space of time intervened between the communication of her intention and the carrying of it into execution, for Hepburn to effect a great change both in his life and in his house. Briefly, he married a wealthy wife, and with her money he built him a beautiful mansion on one of the many slopes of Glene, in Somersetshire—a mansion in which a queen might deign to be entertained by her subject, and in which a subject might dare to entertain his queen.

Had such a thing been possible, the Hepburn of the Elizabethan period would have stamped the building with his own lineaments. As this was an architectural feat which no one cared to undertake, he was content with stamping it with his individuality to the degree of building the south front in the form of the initial letter of his name.

Glene, the house itself, was beautifully situated. It was built on a piece of table-land that came in the middle of a long sweep of sloping ground, which stretched away above and below the house to a great extent.

Now in the days when this story commences, the south front, the " H " of Hepburn, was veiled and draped with a luxuriant growth of roses, whose branches had assumed the dimensions of trees, magnolias, jasmine, myrtles, and other shrubs, which had seen three or four generations born and buried. The battlemented summit of the mansion was crowned with rich red and white blooms in summer; the quaint, heavily-bastioned windows were darkened by them. It was the best horticultural show she had seen for the season, young Mrs. Hepburn thought, as the carriage that brought her—a bride—to her new home, wheeled round to the south front, and pulled up at the iron-bound little black oak-door which opened into the hall.

The housekeeper, Mrs. Bingham, the widow of a man who had been land-steward to Mr. Hepburn's predecessor at Glene, had ranged the servants in an imposing-looking phalanx to receive and welcome their new mistress. After their several manners, these servants strove to look the gladness and welcome which they must not speak, and were supposed to feel, as the young lady—the bride whom their master had brought home—stepped out of his carriage, and entered her husband's house for the first time. But Amelia had no glad looks and no gratitude for the welcome to express in return. " She was a handsome young lady, tall, and a fine figure of a woman, and beautifully dressed, and she looked almost too tired to smile." That was all the servants could say about her yet.

In truth she was very tired—very tired, indeed—strong as were her muscles, and sound as was her constitution. For all her hard and practical nature, and profoundly sensible way of looking at things, she had indulged in a few hopes and illusions which the experience of her married life, short as it had been, had proved to be empty as air, and false as a mirage. She had married an old man, after having made great concessions to him during the time of her engagement; married him with some sort of hope that she would be well recompensed for what some people deemed the sacrifice she had made. This hope had been disappointed— crushed out from the very first. He was kind, and he was fond. But his fondness she would gladly have bartered for more indulgence and greater freedom. He was an old man, but by no means a doting and easily led old man.

She had thought to win the most absolute trust and confidence from him by that offer she had made respecting the terms on which she should enjoy her jointure, did he die and leave her. He had accepted and acted upon that offer gratefully at the time; but now he seemed to think that it was only the right and proper thing for her to have made it, and she purchased no privileges by it, but had just "given it for nothing," she told herself, ill-temperedly. She had not enjoyed her honeymoon. On the contrary, she had been more unhappy and discontented during that first month of her married life than she had ever been in all her life before. She had longed to taste the fruits of the wealth for which she had married a man who was a year or two older than her father. She longed to travel luxuriously, and to be remarkable in some of the gayest cities of the world, for her state and splendour, and her youth, in sharp contrast to his age. But he disregarded this longing, even when she hinted at it plainly. Excitement and Continental cookery disagreed with him; he told her, moreover, he thought that "two people who

were to be all in all to each other while they
lived, stood a better chance of becoming ac-
quainted in solitude than in society." Accordingly he carried her away to a secluded spot,
near Derwentwater, quite out of the tourists'
track, and stayed there until Amelia hated the
Lake district and all connected with it.'

He was a man of a polished manner—
polished with the polish of fifty years ago.
He was cheerful in temperament, unaccustomed
to change, and desirous of no greater breaks
in the monotony of their lives than little evening strolls with Amelia by the lake-side. The
way in which he ate the bread of cheerfulness,
and drank the new milk of cows in this quiet
farm-house, in which he had secured lodgings,
irritated and depressed the young lady he had
married, to a degree she dared not show as yet.

" How bored you must be here after the life
you lead at Glene," she broke out abruptly one
night, as she was sauntering by his side, tired,
weary, and intensely disgusted with the length
of a story void of point, which he had been
telling her.

" The life I have led at Glene is not much

gayer than this, and far less happy, for I have not had you there," he said, gallantly, and Amelia shuddered as she listened, and felt what a prospect this shadowed forth.

" But it must be better there," she told herself, hoping against hope. " We must know a lot of people, and there will be something more to do than to pick up mosses, and grub after ferns. I shall die of him and myself, if we stay here much longer."

After this it will readily be understood why she could not respond more heartily than she did to the welcome given her by the Glene household. She was very doubtful of them and of herself—doubtful of their having the power, or the knowledge, or the freedom of will to be conducive to the furthering of that gorgeous comfort, and ostentatious luxury, for the enjoyment of which she had married Mr. Hepburn.

All the details of that first evening at Glene grated upon her harshly. They had been married a month now, and this coming home of hers took place in July, the month of roses. Glene never looked better at any time of the

year than it did at this season, which Mr.
Hepburn had selected as the one in which to
introduce it and its new mistress to one another. But Amelia, though her heart would
swell with elation one moment at the thought
of reigning over this beautiful old place, would
suffer sullen doubt, and the expression of sullen
doubt, to cloud both heart and countenance
the next moment, as the fear that her rule
would be but a cramped and fettered one
assailed her.

So many things jarred upon the habit of
mind of the girl who had lived the quick,
ever-changing life that is lived by the daughters
of wealthy, indulgent people in the gay metro-
politan suburbs.   It has been said that Amelia
never had wasted any of her time in flirtations of
an unremunerative order, but she had otherwise
lived the modernised edition of a young lady's
career.   Consequently, the even tenour of the
way in which it was evident Mr. Hepburn was
accustomed to go, loomed tamely and insuffi-
ciently before her.

She got out of the carriage and went into
the house, though he asked her to stay a mo-

ment to look at an enormous blush-rose tree in full bloom, which he had planted when he first came to Glene as the owner of it, three or four-and-thirty years ago. " Fussing about a rose the instant he comes home," his wife thought, angrily, as she threw one scornful glance towards the tree at which he was pointing with her sunshade; " and carrying an umbrella, too, as if he did not look enough like an old fogey without that." She would not wait to see how gladly and respectfully, and withal heartily, his household welcomed him when he came on into the house at last. She might have forgiven his fussing about his rose-tree, and looking an old fogey, if she had noted the kindly, well-bred courtesy which made him remember something that was dear or interesting to the meanest in his house, and mention it as if it were interesting to him. But she would not wait ; she had gone on, asking impatiently to be " shown to her room," whither she and her maid quickly wended their way, too much put out at his having had a thought of anything beyond showing her off proudly and triumph-antly, to betray the curiosity and admiration she felt about the stately mansion through which she was passing.

Presently she put on a loose wrapper, and sent down word to Mr. Hepburn that she " hoped he would excuse her, and sit down to dinner without her ; she was tired." A message from him in return begged her to exert herself sufficiently to dress and come down. And she had lived with him long enough to feel that she had better do as he desired. When she went down at length, she found him awaiting her in evening dress, and actually—already disregarding the conventional privacy of a bride's first evening at home—by his side stood Mr. Scorrier. So she wrapped herself in a gloomy and grand silence, which they did not seem to remark, but talked themselves, rather cheerfully than otherwise, of agricultural and local matters, steering clear of all mention of the great names of the county, which she had carefully learnt from " Dodd's Landed Gentry."

"When you know what a dull little place Danebury is, you will understand how rejoiced I was to see your carriage bringing you home to-night, Mrs. Hepburn," Mr. Scorrier said to

her, when the ice had been melted a little by
aid of the wine. The remark made Mrs. Hepburn gather up her gloves and her irritable pride,
and prepare to withdraw herself. But even
when she was alone in the big drawing-room—
which it would be no affectation to dignify by
the name of saloon in her future letters to
former envious and curious friends—even when
she was alone, with everything that was beautiful about her, she could not get over the smarting
sensation which Mr. Scorrier's remark had
caused her to feel. Apparently her advent had
been of importance to him, and to him alone,
as an event that was likely to break the monotony of his life. But how about the monotony
of hers? Why it was better that such monotony should remain unbroken, mortification-en-
gendering as it was, than it should be relieved
only by one whom she was resolved to regard
and treat as an inferior.

That her husband had a warm feeling of
regard for the young Danebury surgeon; that
Mr. Scorrier, if her husband's will was carried
out, would be a frequent and an honoured guest
at Glene; and that she would be compelled to

treat him with a civility in which there should
be no half-hidden sting of superiority; all this
was, and must be. If he had been the son of
some noble, noted, or honourable house, no
amount of brainlessness or worthlessness would
have been drawbacks to the intimacy in her
eyes; but, as it was, he was only a surgeon—
only a young, unknown, clever, gentlemanly
country surgeon; and she was one of those self-
punishing creatures—a woman who was always
uncertain about, and anxious to make good and
secure, her social status. The dread that an
intimacy or even an acquaintanceship with one
a little beneath her might affect her claims on
the consideration to be gained at any price of
any one a little above her, had been about
Amelia all her life. That this anxiety should
rob her of all tact and discrimination, and cause
her to blunder very often, was only natural.
She did not possess the seldom-failing test which
is inherent in the gentlewoman born and bred,
by which the true metal can be detected from
the base. She would hover about too long on
the debateable ground, waiting for some one
about whom even she felt assured to show her

what was the safe line of conduct to be pursued with regard to some new acquaintance. And then she would follow the path shown with undue avidity, or avoid it altogether in servile imitation, as only a treacherous narrow-natured woman can. Yet with all these blemishes of bad breeding in her character, she was so coldly, quietly correct in manners and ideas, that she invariably gained from those who knew but little of her, the reputation of being " a nice, ladylike girl."

Her dread of compromising herself—of doing anything that might lead even the servants to suspect that she had not been born to a state equal to this which surrounded her at Glene, kept her very quiet. She was afraid to seem interested, in fear of being pronounced unaccustomed. So she sat still and was dull, and suffered the longing to go out and look about this kingdom over which she had come to reign, rather than gratify it under the auspices of the housekeeper; sat still and wondered whom she could take as her guide in this strange country, where she had no predecessor's visiting-list to consult, since clearly her husband did not

properly estimate the advantages of his exalted
position.

They sat a long time over their wine that
night. It seemed, even to Mr. Scorrier, who
was not at all too anxious to rejoin the lady of
the house, that they were very long in doing so.
As soon as she had left them, and Mr. Hepburn had seated himself in his chair, Arthur
Scorrier had given way more freely than he had
done before to the pleasure he felt in seeing his
old and kind friend home again. " It has been
hard work for me at Danebury without you, sir,"
he said. " I had constantly to remind myself
that yours was an absence of special happiness
to yourself, in order to bear it patiently."

Mr. Hepburn gave his hand to his guest, and
some of his best claret to himself. " It will be
better for you next year, my boy," he said.
"You will join the hunt this winter, and will
find that the best men in it are men of your own
stamp. Danebury will assume a very different
aspect in your eyes before the year is out."

" My mother has been staying with me while
you were away," Mr. Scorrier said.

" Your mother here ! "

"Yes, while you were away," the young man answered, half apologetically; "she has not moved out of that quiet little home of hers for so many years, that I thought it was a good opportunity of giving her a change."

"I always understood from you that Mrs. Scorrier had a great dislike to travelling, and that she was perfectly happy and satisfied in her place of abode," Mr. Hepburn said, coldly. "I am very much surprised to hear of your having brought her up here for nothing."

"My mother had a not altogether unnatural desire to have a look at what is likely to be my home for many years," Mr. Scorrier replied.

Old Mr. Hepburn threw himself back in his chair, and made an impatient movement with his head, and an exclamation with his tongue that defies spelling.

"Women always want to have a look at what cannot possibly concern them," he said, in a displeased tone; "it was inconsiderate of you to upset your mother—to break into the habit of years, and give her a necessarily brief and unsatisfactory peep into a new life. I should have opposed the scheme, had I been at home."

"Had you been at home, I should not have proposed it," Arthur Scorrier answered. "I respect your disinclination to meet your old friend's widow—though I think it morbid, mind you, sir," he added, eagerly. "My mother wondered why I would not let her have a glance inside Glene, which, of course, I would not do; she has no idea that yours has been a systematic avoidance of her."

Mr. Hepburn smiled urbanely, and nodded his head, in acceptance of the idea of credulity on Mrs. Scorrier's part, which was just shadowed forth in her son's speech.

"In reality, it is a thing that is very immaterial to her, whether I see her or not, and it would be, or rather I will say it *might* be, painful to me. Though so many years have passed, the circumstances of poor Scorrier's death are fresh in my mind as if it had happened yesterday; and while that is the case, I would very much rather not see his widow, your mother. You, and she too, must forgive me the indulgence of this 'morbid fancy,' as you are pleased to call it, Arthur; you must respect it too, if you value my happiness."

He spoke with some emotion, and Arthur Scorrier felt uncomfortable. He had promised his mother, when she left him to go back to her home in Penzance, that he would use his influence with Mr. Hepburn, and get her husband's old friend to meet her face to face. " It would be a comfort to me to see one who saw the last of him, Arthur," the good lady had said, with tears in her eyes, " just to hear if he mentioned me during his last hours; it would be a comfort and a pleasure; and mine has been a hard fate, but for you, my son."

In reply to this little unreasonable burst of craving for a very slight and dubious comfort, Arthur Scorrier had undertaken to mention his mother's visit, casually, and to bring about— not a reconciliation, because there had never been a quarrel—but a fair understanding between his kind old friend and his loving old mother ; and this was the result of it. This disavowal of her, and almost expressed determination to keep her at a distance, was the result of the attempt which he now felt he had been unwise to make.

" I will respect it, in the way you mean,

certainly, sir, as you desire me to do so," he answered, slowly.

" Why, you see," Mr. Hepburn explained, recovering his affability and usually satisfied demeanour in a moment, " a thousand things would make an interview between Mrs. Scorrier and myself painful to me ; at least now particularly. I am just married, just beginning life, with an affectionate and admirable wife. I could not fail to have painful recollections of the time when your father was similarly situated with regard to your mother; and as I am no stoic, my dear boy, I could not stand it."

There was a pause for a few seconds after this, then Mr. Hepburn resumed :

" As for Mrs. Scorrier, or any one else, seeing Glene, you know the great objection I have to making a show of my house. You are as welcome in it, Arthur, as if you were my own son ; but I established the rule of refusing admission to staring strangers when I came here first. Highly as I value all the privileges of my position, perhaps I value my privacy more highly than any other one of them. Shall we go and look for Mrs. Hepburn now, and ask her for a cup of tea?"

"The foibles of old age are rather hard to put up with," Arthur Scorrier thought, shrugging his shoulders, as he followed his host to Amelia's presence; "he seemed to forget that I was a free agent when he was almost scolding me for having had my own mother in my own house." Then the recollection of a long list of systematic benefits and kindnesses received from Mr. Hepburn ever since his boyhood, swept across his mind, and obliterated all feeling of annoyance at the foibles, and the fruits of them.

Opening out from the further end of the drawing-room, there was a large conservatory, filled with the rarest foliage and flower-plants. "It has just been stocked afresh in honour of the bride," Mr. Hepburn said; and Amelia was trying to look gratified at the honour, when her gratification was dashed by her husband asking:

"By the way, Arthur, I hope I did not forestal the completion of your conservatory by sending you those plants down?"

They were at the door of the little palace of glass, looking in upon the gorgeous rows of scented and unscented blooms, as Mr. Hepburn spoke. A sudden desire to seem generous in her husband's eyes, and to show Mr. Scorrier that she too would not object to patronising him, and giving to him out of her abundance, seized upon Amelia. Accordingly she stopped his answering Mr. Hepburn's question immediately, by saying, " Have you a greenhouse, Mr. Scorrier ? I will tell the people to give you some of these plants ; I don't suppose they are too common in Danebury."

" No, they are not too common," Mr. Scorrier said, carelessly. He was ignorant as yet that it was the lady's plan to put him in the position of the obliged inferior. " No, they are not too common, but I am the happy possessor of a very fair show of them."

" I suppose you are not horticulturist enough to know that these are new and rare sorts," Amelia said, lifting her eyebrows in her effort to make him understand that he must have overstated facts in declaring that he had a very fair show of " them."

"Yes, I'm told they are new, and I see they are rare, though I am not much of a horticulturist," he replied. "Mr. Hepburn was kind enough to remember that my conservatory was empty when he was giving the order for yours to be stocked. I hope you will come and see it soon," he continued; "just as though he thought himself my equal, or moved in the same set I shall be in," Mrs. Hepburn said to herself, indignantly, as, without replying to his invitation, she made her way back into the drawing-room.

By-and-by, when Mr. Hepburn was taking her the round of that portion of the house which he found to be easy of access to himself after dinner, they stopped before a portrait of a long past Dame Hepburn, whom Arthur Scorrier declared to be "something like Miss Vargrave." The likeness was not very strong, indeed it could only have been discovered by the eyes of one who was anxious to find it, and use it as a means of mentioning the one to whom it was likened. Still it was strong enough for Mr. Scorrier's purpose.

"There is the same look of gentleness and

power combined about the brow and eyes, that makes Miss Vargrave's face so interesting," he said, appealing to Mrs. Hepburn.

"I don't see it at all," that lady replied. "Cissy Vargrave's forehead is too low for her to have much of what I call 'power,' and, I suppose you mean the same thing, mental power."

" Her forehead isn't high certainly—a high forehead is a ghastly thing in a woman—but it's high enough for plenty of intellect of a fine order."

"It would be a fortunate thing for her if she was as clever as you suppose her to be; she might do something with her brains then to maintain herself. I always think she ought to go out as a governess," Amelia continued, appealing to her husband; " she is really not entitled to be in the position her uncle's mistaken kindness places her in for a time."

" Ah !" Mr. Hepburn rejoined, trying to look interested, "you are speaking of your friend, Miss Vargave."

" I am speaking of Cissy Vargrave. We were never very intimate, only one likes to be

kind to every one; there must be equality in
order to make great intimacy pleasant between
any people—don't you think so, Mr. Scorrier?"

"I am a poor judge of what constitutes
social inequality between middle-class people,"
he said, rather contemptuously; and Mrs.
Hepburn had to remind herself that there was
something undignified in fighting with the
Danebury surgeon's opinions as to caste, in
order to constrain herself to keep silence when
he included her in what she considered such
derogatory mention.

CHAPTER IV.

NUMBER NINE, THE CRESCENT.

THE house, number nine, The Crescent, Penzance, was a model of neatness and respectability, inside and outside. It could be seen by all such as are accustomed to look for causes in results, that it was the home of an elderly lady of comfortable means and unrestrained power to spend the same. A cleanly, well-attended-to little house, with not a detail connected with paint, varnish, and plastering neglected. The curtains that peeped through its vividly fresh, green Venetian blinds were always deeply red in winter, and purely white in summer. Its glass and brass knobs always shone brightly. Its tiny bit of space in front, enclosed within always unbroken railings, was full invariably of the most seasonable and brilliantly tinted flowers. Undriven snow was the example aimed at apparently by the cleaner of its door-steps. It shone down every other house in the curved row of neatly built, two-story houses known as The Crescent, Penzance.

Twenty-eight years ago number nine, The Crescent, had been taken by its present occupant, Mrs. Scorrier, who had come to it in her first great grief, and had got attached to the unpretending little place, and remained in it ever since. Her great grief was the death by drowning, in Mount's Bay (here close to Penzance), of her husband. She had a smaller grief—one that she was very quiet about. But it leaked out in some mysterious way, notwithstanding her reticence, and it was shortly known amongst the current tenants of The Crescent that this husband, whom she lamented so unfeignedly, had never placed a wedding-ring on her finger.

Three or four years before her first appearance in Penzance, Mrs. Scorrier had been living a happy, dull, unromantic, good life in her father's house in one of the eastern counties; for she was pretty, and superior in manner and appearance to the agricultural class to which she belonged; and so she was gaining much honourable and admiring mention from her compeers, when a change came. A gentlemanly tourist saw her, and made love to her; and pretty, gentle, confiding Mabel Wilmot left her home to become the wife of a man who had always some plausible reason to give for not making her such just yet. So matters went on quietly enough until her son was born, and then she pressed her claim with a vigour that startled Mr. Scorrier into promising to attend to and comply with it. With a view to the fulfilment of this promise, he left her in the London suburban home which had been hers since her elopement, and went away to see some members of his family and to consult his men of business. The poor young mother, who was waiting so anxiously to be a wife, took her last leave of him with passionately loving trustfulness. That she had done so was a comfort to her in all her after years, for the next thing she heard of Mr. Scorrier was through Mr. Hepburn's lawyer. Mr. Hepburn had been boating with his old friend, Mr. Scorrier, in Mount's Bay, when the boat had upset, and there was an end of him, and the one who was no wife was widowed.

After a while, the poor, broken lady, whose own family were alienated from her, came down to Penzance, and made her home within reach of the graveyard where was buried the drowned man who had wrecked her life, and been so dear to her. She had come down, and shown herself most unwisely regardless of appearances at first, for she wore a widow's dress, and still suffered the third finger of her left hand to be unadorned by the wife's ring. But as she lived very quietly, as she was sweet and kind to all such as it was in her power to show sweetness and kindness to, the few who had noticed the want forgave it. Then, after a time, before her boy reached years of observation, she strengthened her claim to being considered the legal widow of the man she mourned, by buying a plain gold ring, and putting it on herself, and telling a little fable to her son of the past happy day when his father had given it to her.

She had never sought to get into society, or

made friends, or rendered herself conspicuous, or in any way courted remark and investigation. Accordingly, when the few who had noticed and tattled about her, when she came here first, died out, or moved away, her story was as utterly forgotten as if it had never been whispered, and the new generation who sprang up and dwelt in The Crescent knew her only as the excellent widow-lady whose house always looked so nice. So completely had she lived down rumour and suspicion by a long course of quiet integrity.

Before he had left her on that journey from which he never returned, Mr. Scorrier had provided for her amply. He had made her a gift of money, had paid it into a bank in her name, and had further paid in another sum of ten thousand pounds, to be dedicated to the sole use and service of his son. Consequently, though he died without a will, and without further mention of her, she had no ground of complaint against him on the score of improvidence. He had taken care that she should have enough and to spare. Moreover, Mr. Hepburn wrote to tell her that the interests of

his dead friend's son would always be dear to
him, though he must decline holding any personal communication with herself, giving as a
reason for this avoidance of her "that the
sight of one who had been so dear to, and so
injured by, Mr. Scorrier would be too much for
his mind and nerves, which were painfully and
dangerously sensitive." This reason and the
result of it were alike painful to her. But she
was a patient, enduring, gentle-hearted woman.
So she gratefully accepted all the ki dness
which Mr. Hepburn heaped on Arthur from his
boyhood, and never resented his avoidance of
herself. Even when it came to the critical
question of deciding what was to be Arthur's
career, she consulted the stranger who ignored
her, before she gave voice to her own wishes on
the subject. And when it was settled, when
Arthur had walked the hospitals, and passed
his last examination, she stoutly subdued all
outward signs of sorrow when she found that
Mr. Hepburn's generosity in almost giving
Arthur an excellent practice in and about Danebury would be the means of making her a
stranger in her son's house.

She had always patiently accepted Mr. Hepburn's treatment of herself—patiently accepted it as a sort of tacit moral rebuke and punishment for her youthful dereliction from the path of virtue and propriety; for her early curse in having loved exceedingly unwisely and well. But though she thus patiently accepted it herself, she did sometimes wonder what her son thought about it. It was so very much to her, that the man who had seen the last of the one who had been the husband of her heart, should sit in the seat of the virtuously scornful above her—so very much to her, that she did not quite realize of how very little importance it seemed to the younger mind, in which dwelt no painful knowledge, no suspicion of the reason why. Arthur thought it what he called it—a morbid feeling on the part of Mr. Hepburn—nothing more.

That one little journey up from the bold, beautiful Cornish coast, to the midst of the soft-smiling Somersetshire slopes where her son lived, had been the only break in the placid routine of her life which Mrs. Scorrier had known for twenty-nine years. It had been a very delightful visit, without any drawbacks, unless the slight one of not being able to catch a glimpse of either the interior of Glene or the person of its owner could be counted as such. Arthur's house was very pretty, and his establishment was well-appointed. It seemed to his mother to be conducted on a spacious and grand scale, by comparison with her own two-storey house in The Crescent. Moreover, it appeared to Mrs. Scorrier that she was plunged into a vortex of dissipation while she was Arthur's guest. The handsome young surgeon, who had studied medicine and sundry other things in Paris, Vienna, and Berlin for some years, was very popular in the neighbourhood. Mrs. Scorrier experienced some of the sensations of a *grande dame* when she was rolling in the Danebury fly to a dinner-party at some place in the vicinity. She experienced them even more fully when the owners and occupants of these places rolled in return to her son's house ; for Arthur had a fine taste in giving dinners, and people were very glad to go to him.

But now the season of dissipation was over,

and she was back at number nine, alone with
her two middle-aged servants, and her one
middle-aged spaniel again. The days at Danebury had been very bright, so bright that she
had been dazzled out of all thought of the
great expense at which Arthur must be living.
But now the days were past, and she had time
to think and to fear.

It had taken some time for her to settle down
and resume old habits after this great event.
Not that she was an excitable or feverish-
minded woman, but because she fancied she
had a great deal to do after an absence from
home. Her servants were trustworthy; still
it was a point of duty with her to go over the
contents of the linen-trunk and small plate-
closet, list in hand, before she could con-
scientiously pronounce that all was right.
Then she had a few visits of ceremony to
receive and make on a few intimate friends,
who marked their sense of the glories in which
she had been participating, by coming in their
best bonnets and clothes, and speaking in de-
preciatory—not to say contemptuous—terms of
Penzance and the society they knew.

It was so delightful to the poor woman who had been weak, but never wicked, and who had waited so patiently, and fought such a quiet unpretending little fight for consideration and honour—it was so delightful to her to speak out in open proud terms of her son and his successes. To talk of his possible marriage with some girl of degree, of whom she, his mother, might speak " as one of the so-and-so's," and in whom she might glory as in one who added glory to her son. It was the dream of her life that Arthur should marry well ; that he should marry some woman with a stainless name. The dream of her life—her nightly prayer—the one thought which she had pondered over and cultivated from the birth of her boy. Worldly consideration and respectability were as dear to the heart of this woman, who had sacrificed them to love in her youth, as they were to the master of Glene, who would not meet her, because—she felt that was the reason—because he could not hold his hand out to one who had been but the mistress of his friend.

As has been said, her story had died out

now; but even if it had not done so, who could have judged her harshly, or even smiled cynically, as she sat and prophesied about her son? She was sitting in her little drawing-room, a perfect temple of purity and cleanliness, surrounded by a few friends, discoursing about Arthur and the esteem he was held in. The hot August air was coming in at the open window, its fierceness slightly tempered now by the fresh evening sea-breeze. A few people had come away from the broiling open parade to walk in the shade of the trees that grew in The Crescent, and amongst the number was a party of four, two of whom were young ladies, and very pretty. The old ladies assembled in Mrs. Scorrier's room gathered round the window to look at this group, and one of them remarked, "How full Penzance is of pretty girls just now! Mr. Arthur should find time to come home; or has he any counter-attraction?"

"I don't think there is at present, but I should set my face against any watering-place young lady as a wife for my son; you never know who people are, and it does behove young men to be so careful."

"Still it is so much better that a medical man should be married, that you will not be sorry to hear he has found a wife," another lady said.

"No, rejoiced; for I am convinced Arthur will choose wisely," his mother said. "So much depends on a wife; she makes or mars a man; but my boy can only choose well; he is so good."

Meanwhile the party of four, evidently strangers, judging from the way they looked about them, passed and repassed the window several times. "Backwards and forwards here, in front of the dove-coloured old lady's abode, if you please, uncle!" the prettier of the two girls said, when the uncle appealed to suggested extending their promenade beyond the limit of the terrace. "She's a picture of peace, and I like looking at her; besides, her mignonette reminds me of London."

"Out of which you were most impatient to get—please remember that, Cissy," the other girl remarked.

"Yes, I know I was. Amelia's wedding put the finishing-stroke to my hardly sustained endurance this summer; but that is no reason why I should not like the mignonette."

"Didn't Mr. Scorrier tell us that his mother lived in The Crescent?" Isabelle said, abruptly. "Of course, this is The Crescent."

"And of course my embodiment of peace in the dove-coloured satin is his mother," Cissy said, carelessly; "and it was in the hope of seeing her that I urged coming to Penzance— that is the train of argument running through your mind, I know, Isabelle."

"I wonder if Amelia and Mr. Hepburn will meet us here, as Amelia promised," Isabelle said, avoiding answering her cousin's remark.

"I hope, if they do, that Penzance will seriously disagree with your father and mother, in order that we may flee at once; she would be worse than a croquet-party at her mother's."

"Will you never stay with her at Glene, Cissy, after all that has been said about our going?"

"No, never," Cissy answered, rather quickly.

"I believe it would be pleasant," Isabelle

urged, "because Amelia would never be able to give herself airs to us."

"I couldn't stay in her house, and see her give herself airs to anybody," Cissy replied.

"Why? you needn't care about the people down there, and it would be a nice house to stay in. I can't think what has set you so against going."

"Her impertinence to Mr. Scorrier." And the words fell upon the ears of Mr. Scorrier's mother. "I couldn't stay in her house and witness it, and as I don't care to come out in the character of a female Quixote, and fight either a troop of asses or windmills, I shall keep out of temptation. I shall stay away from Glene."

"Did you hear that young lady—the darker one of the two—mention any one's name?" Mrs. Scorrier asked, turning her gentle face, now slightly flushed, back towards her friends. "My son's name and Glene—looks an aristocrat—every inch of her." And then the ladies leant as far as they could out of the balconied window, and watched the graceful form of Cissy Vargrave as long as it remained in sight.

Who could it be? The question occupied
all Mrs. Scorrier's waking hours that night.
Who could it be? and how would it be if her
boy loved the lady and the lady loved her boy?
"An aristocrat, every inch of her." Probably
a member of some old Somersetshire family,
and a friend of Mr. Hepburn's. There was an
unmistakeable tone of angry resentment in this
girl's voice when she had spoken about "some
one's impertinence to Mr. Scorrier." "She
would be a wife for him to be proud of, indeed,"
Mrs. Scorrier thought, suffering her imagination to run away with her. "A wife for him
to be proud of—a proper mother for his children. I have always felt that I owe it to
Arthur never to give my consent to his marrying beneath him; I must find out who these
people are, and give a hint to Arthur; such
things are often brought to a happy climax by
a timely word."

The following day Mrs. Scorrier went out
with all the importance of having a special
mission about her. She haunted the principal
shops down near the Parade long after the
marketing was over, in the hope of seeing the

distinguished strangers pass. At length, just as she had suffered herself to drift into the purchase of a serpentine goblet, for which she had no earthly use, the Vargraves came into the shop, and Mrs. Scorrier heard them give a large order, and direct that the things should be sent to " Mr. Vargrave, at the Queen's." " A lovely face and a good name," the old lady thought, heaving a sigh of satisfaction as they departed. " Mr. Digby is attending some one at the Queen's. I'll get him to look at the visitors' book and see where they are from; most likely they have a place near Danebury, though I never heard Arthur mention them." Acting on this belief, Mrs. Scorrier wrote to her son before she saw Mr. Digby, her doctor, and after expatiating on the beauty and grace of a girl whom she had just seen, she went on to tell him that she had just found out that the girl's name was Vargrave, and that she had tried to find it out in consequence of having heard her (the girl) speak in the "most flattering terms of Arthur when passing through The Crescent the night before." " At any rate, that letter can do no harm," Mrs. Scorrier thought, as she sealed and directed it. " And if it's any one some people may consider above him, it will give him confidence to approach her." Mrs. Scorrier prided herself much about this little display of tact and worldly wisdom which she was making. Further, she prided herself on the discrimination she had shown, in at once detecting that " there was something very superior" about the young lady who had been noticed by her outside the window of number nine. Vargrave was a well-sounding name, and she had no doubt about its being a good and old name. A faint hope arose in her heart, that her own family, the brothers and sisters who had cut her because she had disgraced them—(how she shivered even now, as she remembered the terms in which her affectionate relatives had upbraided her for that disgrace which she had brought upon them unwittingly, and unwillingly, poor creature !) a faint hope arose in her mind now, that they would come back to her kindly. Come back to her kindly, and own her as one of them, and give her again, after long years of loneliness and estrangement, the proud, safe feeling of belonging to, of being of kin to, the Wilmots. They would be sure to do this when she could write and tell that her son had married a lady of name and repute, whose antecedents were all good, and who might be honourably mentioned before all men. Poor old lady! she trembled with pleasure and hope, as she thought of all that her son's marriage might do for her. For these years of solitude had only deadened, not killed, the family feeling. And she felt that though all social odium had long ago been lived down by her, the sting of having felt it once would never be quite eradicated, until she had been received with respect, if not with honour, in that old eastern country homestead where she had been born. And this would be, she felt sure that it would be, when Arthur had won some highly-born young lady for his wife, and that wife had owned her as a mother. Mrs. Scorrier drew a deep, grateful, thankful breath as she told herself that her long career of patient, quiet endurance, had not been a penance vain for the fault and folly that was less hers than another's.

Meanwhile, the fair foundation on whom

this fabric of hope and pride was built, was
having a very turbulent time of it in her own
feelings. The subject of the autumn campaign
had, as usual, been largely discussed in family
council before any definite plan was formed.
Change of air and scene, and consequently
change of custom and diet and thought, were
essential to them; for they were all pretty
well worn out with their share of the London
season. Still, essential as change was to the
constitution of the family, Mr. Vargrave felt it
to be even more essential, in the present
rickety state of finance, that his balance at his
banker's should be a considerable one. And
this balance was severely affected by the dressing and driving, and riding and dancing,
which had been going on for the good of the
girls during the last twelve months. "A short
time abroad would do wonders for us all,"
Mrs. Vargrave had plaintively suggested;
"and one may live very inexpensively in
Paris, and for next to nothing at some places
on the Rhine."

"I think we will defer a scheme of economy
to be carried out at the Grand Hotel until next

year," said her husband ; " and while I am on the subject I may as well make the same remark about Brighton and Scotland. I'll have no going to stay at some Highland shooting-lodge that will involve twelve new evening dresses a-piece."

" Let us go to the Land's End," Cissy said, suddenly. Apparently she had taken no interest in the conversation before it reached this point. " Let us go to the Land's End, Uncle James. There is a cheap and secluded sound about the name of that locality. I shouldn't think people even dined there, much less dressed for dinner."

" Dreadfully out of the way, and we shall never see a soul," Mrs. Vargrave objected. " Oh dear ! I made quite sure that the interest of that legacy would have given us a good treat abroad this year."

" That legacy " was a fair sum left to Mrs. Vargrave, in the spring, by a cousin of hers. On the strength of the interest of it paying for everything she could ever want, she had already dipped deeply into the principal. But as this was a weakness with which he was perfectly familiar, her husband only called her attention to the fact now, by saying—

"I am afraid you must lower your flag. We will gratefully accept something less magnificent than a treat abroad at your hands— say the payment of your own fare down to the Land's End."

" And that will be to Penzance," Cissy said, quietly. " Why not turn a joke into real earnest, Uncle James ? "

" What is that we have been hearing lately about Penzance ?" Mrs. Vargrave said, knitting her brow in vain endeavour to recollect something vague.

" That a great many pilchards and mackerel are caught there," Cissy answered, calmly.

" I believe mamma means that Mr. Scorrier's mother lives there," Isabelle said, laughing.

" Ah ! the pilchard and mackerel fact is the more interesting of the two, you see," Cissy replied, looking her cousin full in the face ; " we can live for 'next to nothing,' as Aunt says of the Rhine towns, upon them."

" I shall tell Amelia we are going to Penzance, if papa decides to go there," Isabelle replied; "it would be nicer if they met us there."

"It would quite do away with both the pleasure and the pilchards," Cissy said, half laughing.

"And it would oblige you girls to have very different sea-side dresses, if Mrs. Hepburn meets us, from what you will want if alone there," Mrs. Vargrave put in, eagerly. "I would not give my consent to your appearing in those blue serges if Amelia is to be there—not for a moment! You must have white ones. I saw some at Marshall and Snelgrove's the other day that will be the very thing for you; that shall be my little present to you girls out of the legacy, as I can't give you the trip abroad."

So finally it was settled that the Vargraves should try Penzance this year, for a change. And as Isabelle carried her design into execution of asking Mrs. Hepburn to join them there, it came about that Arthur Scorrier knew Cissy was there before he received his mother's letter. Much as he wanted to see Cissy again, keenly as he remembered her and

all her charms, and dearly as he would have
liked to find out without delay whether or not
he was as keenly remembered by her, he could
not leave Danebury. His professional obligations bound him to remain, and so he could
only respond warmly to his mother's eulogium
on the beautiful girl who had mentioned his
name flatteringly in The Crescent, and hope
that Miss Cissy Vargrave would soon be
staying at Glene. While there was a chance
of Cissy's coming there, he resolved to keep
the peace with Mrs. Hepburn, though that lady
in some of her phases was very hard to bear.
He would not have been so tolerant to her as
he was, had he not seen that the husband regarded him as warmly and well as the wife did
coldly and ill. Still, had it not been for the
thought that it would be pleasant to have free
ingress into the house, should Miss Vargrave
come there to stay, Amelia would have carried
her point, and Mr. Scorrier and Glene would
have lapsed asunder. Not that she disliked
him personally; but she did look upon him as
a barrier between herself and the great people
whom she was sighing to know on equal terms.

As yet these had only come about her gradually and with caution, in a way that did not pledge them to further intimacy, and she looked for the cause of this guarded caution in the wrong direction.

CHAPTER V.

MRS. HEPBURN'S CONDESCENSION.

On the whole, looking at the matter from the point of view that had been hers while she was still Miss Foster, living in No. —, Ladbroke Square, Bayswater, Amelia saw her marriage was a mistake. She was not given the opportunity of flaunting herself in the gay light in which she would have been visible to former friends and acquaintances, and new people did not come about her to be dazzled with the lightning rapidity which she had attributed to them in anticipation. Before she had been resident at Glene for one week, she discovered that, if she was to be a happy woman, it must be in Mr. Hepburn's way, not in her own.

And his was a very quiet, uninteresting

way. It had come to be an understood thing in
the neighbourhood that Mr. Hepburn did not
care for society, and so would not attend to its
calls, and repay it for any time, trouble, or
expense bestowed upon him. He had gone on
in his uneventful, unpretending course so long,
that even now, when he married a young wife,
no one thought that it would be either prac-
ticable or worth while to attempt to move him
out of it. The owners of adjacent places
" supposed they must call on the young wife,"
and did call, after a time. But she was not
the type of young wife whom they had expected to see, and so they pronounced her a
failure in most cases. She was a hard, al-
culating, town-bred girl, of the second order,
and she was palpably anxious to take her
place—the place that was hers by right of
her husband—amongst them. Naturally this
anxiety made her feel the time they kept her
waiting, before they indicated their willingness
for her to take this place, very long and weary.
Day after day, Glene and all its beauties grew
to be more and more tedious in her eyes, and
the aggravation of her spirit was increased by

the satisfaction she saw Mr. Hepburn felt in his marriage not having broken up his long routine of quietness.

It was worse, ten times worse, than the dreary time at the lake-side farm-house, for then she had the prospect of a change to look forward to ; while here, now that the looked-for change had come, there was nothing beyond it. It was in vain that she told herself constantly that he must soon, in reason, remember his age and her youth. He never seemed to have a thought of the latter fact. There was an elderly comfortableness about all his arrangements, but there was no provision made for a possible burst of youthful exuberance of spirits on her side.

She put herself in open opposition to him for the first time on the receipt of an invitation to a large dinner and ball that was to be given at Castlenau. Castlenau was the court of that division of the county, the seat of a great nobleman, the Earl of Ellington, whose second son, the Honourable Walter Bracey, desired to represent the political views of those who were Conservative-minded at the forthcoming election. Mrs. Hepburn soon found out that to visit at Castlenau was a great thing, and that not to visit at Castlenau was oblivion. Accordingly now she strenuously advocated the acceptance of this invitation, and Mr. Hepburn just as strenuously opposed it.

" I shall feel that I am a mere nobody if I am not there," she said, in an injured tone.

" You are more likely to feel yourself a mere nobody if you do go," he replied. " Walter Bracey will have found out before that time that I don't mean to support him, and this is, as I tell you, a purely political affair; besides, the woman hasn't even called on you."

" What woman ?" Amelia asked.

" Why, Lady Ellington," Mr. Hepburn replied, in rather a louder key than he usually spoke in; " a woman who, if she wasn't in the peerage, would be black-balled in respectable society."

" She sent her card, if she didn't call in person," Amelia said, angrily; " and I'm sure I for one can forgive any one doing that in preference to driving twenty miles."

"Then I really wonder at you being so anxious to drive twenty miles to dine and dance before her, in return for the dubious honour."

"Can't you understand that it is dull for me here sometimes, Mr. Hepburn? I have not outlived all taste for pleasure," Amelia answered, bitterly.

"But I fail to see what pleasure you can have at Castlenau," Mr. Hepburn argued, brightly. "I have told you my opinion of the lady who would be your hostess. I have more than hinted that her attentions to you have been tardy, and that now they are paid, they are due to a cause which is not flattering to you. It is quite past my comprehension how you can care to go."

"Everybody's attentions have been tardy, as far as that goes," Amelia said, suddenly. "I detest morning calls from people who have nothing to say to me, and to whom I have nothing to say, and morning calls have been my only taste of society since I came down here."

"Yes," Mr. Hepburn said, in a well-satisfied tone; "it is, I think, pretty generally known that I dislike miscellaneous visiting; the few friends I have are true, and you will, I hope, soon appreciate them as fully as they deserve to be appreciated."

" My being civil to old Mrs. Pottinger and her daughters needn't prevent my going to Castlenau," Amelia urged.

Mrs. Pottinger was the widow of the late Rector of Danebury, and, with three or four unmarried daughters, still lived on in the village. They were some of the sharpest thorns in Amelia's flesh, for they had the painful habit of dropping in at Glene very often, and of never having anything fresh to say. But they were really good, genuine people—people who, to Mr. Hepburn's certain knowledge, had led pious, praiseworthy lives for the last thirty years, under troubles that had sometimes threatened almost to swamp them. Mrs. Pottinger had been left a widow, with a large family, and little to live upon, just as the bloom and interest of youth fled from her. She was neither a clever woman nor a worldly woman; but she was sensible in a practical, straightforward way, that seemed to be an infinitely commendable thing in Mr. Hepburn's eyes. The art of pushing was one that she had never learnt, and that was utterly beyond her practising by intuition; but she had a great gift of gentleness, and a power of patience. And these two qualities had actually endeared her to the man who lacked both gentleness and patience himself, but who prized them above all other attributes in women.

Accordingly a real, thorough friendship existed between the master of Glene and the inhabitants of the little trellis-covered house in the village, where Mrs. Pottinger and her daughters lived. For years the ladies, to whom his wife found it so hard to be civil even, had been his chief advisers and almoners in the matter of all parochial charities. Long ago his kindness to, and interest in, her and her children had caused Mrs. Pottinger to make a mistake. But she made it in her own mind alone, and no one but herself knew that a few of the days of her monotonous existence had been brightened by the hope of being mistress of Glene. But now she had banished the very memory of that mistake. There were no back-thoughts, no lamentations over what might have been had she been younger and fairer, and Mr. Hepburn more susceptible, to make her other than she seemed—a most loyal and sincere friend to Amelia. But Amelia was one of those in whose nature it is to turn' a cold shoulder to every good feeling evinced towards them which does not add in any way to their lustre or importance. The sent card of Lady Ellington was a treasure of far greater value in the eyes of Mrs. Hepburn of Glene, than the kindliest acts of heart-courtesy and interest from the unimportant widow.

Unfortunately for herself, Mrs. Hepburn had not the art to conceal her hopes and fears, her small ambitions and disappointments. Thousands of women feel them—act upon them— suffer by them. But to the few only is it given to live as though they felt them not. She was a cold-natured, calculating girl. But her cool nature and calculating spirit led her into the commission of as great social errors as the most hot-headed perversity could have done. The strongest element in her character was subserviency, and this led her to do all sorts of

things that seemed expedient to the shallow
judgment that dared not be free. In her unmarried days she had always regulated her
friendship and acquaintanceship by a very
simple rule. Those who were blessed enough
to find favour in the sight of such as were
recognized as her social superiors by Amelia,
were civilly treated by her also. Those whom
the great ignored, she ignored too, in the
presence of the great. This was her simple,
unvarying rule, and she was pleased to believe
that it had answered very fairly.

On the morning of the day after the receipt
of the invitation to Castlenau, Mrs. Hepburn
was sitting out on the lawn, under the shade of
a huge, sweeping copper-beech. She was very
well pleased just now, for she had carried her
point, and she was gratified and almost happy
in the consciousness that she was going to
"dine and dance," as her husband phrased it,
before Lady Ellington on this day fortnight.
Intuition told her that she would not enjoy
herself as a guest to the manner born would
do. But at least she could profess to enjoy
herself, and she could impress the fact of her

doing so upon less well-endowed friends who
were not allowed to enter into the secret recess
of her mind. Lady Ellington, as her hostess,
could not slight her. Amelia was one of those
people who are self-punishing to this degree,
that they are always anticipating slights.
Lady Ellington could not slight her; and if
other people did—well! there would be no
need to mention it. It will be seen that her
own pretentiousness and mean pride were her
surest foes. No one would have treated her
as, in her self-flagellating imagination, she pic-
tured herself treated.

But this morning she was feeling specially
satisfied, happy, and well assured. She was
arranging sentences in a letter which she intended writing to Cissy Vargrave the day after
her Castlenau campaign—a letter in which the
great event should be so touched upon that
Cissy should believe it to be one of many.
During all the years of their intercourse, Mr.
Vargrave's orphan niece, about whom Amelia
had always been careful to speak slightingly
whenever she mentioned her (Cissy) to strangers, was the one whom it had been Miss

Foster's chiefest aim to impress. Now, though things were changed and Amelia was well established, and Cissy was as insecure socially as ever, this aim still lived and flourished, and caused Mrs. Hepburn to be torn by conflicting feelings. For while she was desirous on the other hand of getting Cissy to Glene and crushing her, so to say, by the sight of Glene grandeur, she could not bear that Cissy should see that Glene grandeur was rather a sad and solitary thing.

As she sat there, giving as deep and serious thought to the matter as if it had been a really deep and serious thing in itself, a shadow crossed the line of sunbeams on which she was gazing out abstractedly, and, looking up, she saw Mr. Scorrier coming towards her. It almost seemed lately that there had been a better feeling between this pair. The lady had ceased from her hitherto incessant attempts to make him feel his position to be less worthy than it was, or less worthy than she thought the position occupied by the friends of Mr. Hepburn of Glene should be. And he accepted the change in her easily enough. Accepted it principally

out of liking and regard for her husband, and
a little because she was a young, good-looking
woman, with a possibility of agreeableness
about her if she liked, and a great deal because
she was a probable means of his again meeting
Miss Vargrave. So now, when he saw her on
the lawn, he turned towards her instead of pursuing his path into the house in search of Mr.
Hepburn, as he had at first intended. When
he neared her he raised his hat, and the sun
fell down lavishly upon his bright fair hair, and
rendered his smiles radiant, and she remembered how her husband looked, and how young
she was, and how, after all, Cissy Vargrave
would have the best of it, if this thing came to
pass.

The thought, and the annoyance it caused
her, made her face flush, and gave her altogether
a warmer air than she was wont to have, when
she gave him her hand, and said, " Good morning." This unusual warmth encouraged him
to speak of something that was near his heart.

" Have you given up the idea of going to
Penzance this month?" he asked. " I hear
from my mother that your friends the Var-

graves are there, and I remember you spoke of going there at one time."

"How does your mother know the Vargraves?" she replied, disregarding his question.

He laughed. "That fact requires a little explanation. My mother lives such a very quiet, uneventful life, that she has got into a habit of noticing trifles and associating them with other trifles—what ladies call putting two and two together, I believe; she was sitting at her window the other night, and she heard some people, in passing, mention Glene and me, and the next day she found out these people to be the Vargraves."

"Glene and you! Do the Vargraves think you live at Glene?" Amelia said, with a little, cross laugh.

"Scarcely that," he answered, carelessly. "Can't you fancy an Eton apothecary being mentioned by the misguided in the same breath with Windsor Castle? But you did not tell me —are you going to join the Vargraves at Penzance?"

"No; it's impossible now," she said, shortly,

feeling that she was wronged in some way by
his allusion to an Eton apothecary and Windsor Castle. "No; it's impossible now. I
have a great many engagements this week; and
the week after we are bound to go to Castlenau, though I should have infinitely have preferred sands and sea-breezes."

"I almost wonder at Mr. Hepburn going
there," Arthur Scorrier said, gravely.

She shrugged her shoulders as if she implied
that the exigencies of their position must of
necessity be sealed books to Mr. Scorrier.

"Because it's a regular transparent bit of
popularity-seeking," Mr. Scorrier went on;
" and Walter Bracey is not the man we want,
or the man Mr. Hepburn would support at all."

"But this affair is quite outside politics,"
said Mrs. Hepburn; "of course people who
don't visit at Castleneau put down everything
that goes on there now to political purposes;
but, as Mrs. Walter Bracey was saying the
other day, when she was over with me, dear
Lady Ellington is a girl at heart still, and
delights in giving a ball as much as her
youngest daughter does. 1 wish," Mrs. Hep-

burn continued, with a sudden access of crushing magnanimity, " that we could get you an
invitation ; I am always sorry when young
men are debarred from anything of the sort."

" You're very kind," he said, drily ; and
Mrs. Hepburn fancied he was smiling.

" When the Castlenau people come to us I
shall ask you to meet them," she said, presently ; and again, as he was impatient to turn
the conversation back to the Cissy Vargrave
topic, he only said, " You are very kind."

Presently, as he sat there gazing abstractedly
down at the grass at his feet, and wondering
how he could most easily revert to the subject
that was most interesting to him, Amelia stole
a glance at him from under her pale lashes—a
sly, cautious glance, that could not be quarrelled
with even if it was caught, but that would
leave an unpleasant impression of having been
watched and measured on the one who was
conscious of it ; the glance that only a deceit-
ful, demure, safe woman can give.

" Did you ask me if Cissy Vargrave was
coming here to stay ? " she asked, slowly.

He started and looked up, but her glance

was averted, and he only saw a very composed, demure, rather sad face, bent towards the earth meditatively.

"No; I hadn't asked you, but I was going to do so," he answered.

She shook her head. "I am afraid not. I don't see how I well can have her here, consistently with what I consider my duty. I have a very high idea of what we women owe to the men we marry, Mr. Scorrier; and though I like Cissy Vargrave for herself, I owe it to my husband to quell that liking and not bring her into his house."

She had a feeling—a hope—as she said this, that she was doing more than enunciating proper views. What the feeling was, or in what it had its rise, she could not tell. She only fancied that if this dawning interest for Cissy, which Mr. Scorrier was displaying, could be crushed, it would be a very good thing. Why it would be a good thing she did not stay to ask herself. It was merely a momentary feeling, and she obeyed it, because it agreed with some previous feeling, which again she did not stay to define as jealousy.

"Are you speaking of Miss Vargrave—your friend?" he asked, when the meaning of her words struck him.

"Yes," she said, still averting her eyes from his. "You see the mistress of such a house as this has responsibilities; I could not reconcile it to my conscience to bring Cecile into a fresh fastidious society that would be sure continually to question who and what she was. Papa and mamma were so good-natured, and liked and respected her uncle so much, that they disregarded all that sort of thing—so would I, if I were still in London; but here, where people have time to think about things, and ask questions, I should compromise myself."

"You will never do that, Mrs. Hepburn," he said, jumping up; and again, as he took off his hat in farewell salute to her, the sun fell down and rendered him radiant, and she remembered that her husband was old and feeble, and saw that this man who had wearied her with questions concerning Cissy was in the prime of his bloom and manhood. "You will never do that, Mrs. Hepburn." She could not determine whether he meant commendation or not.

It was dull and tedious sitting there when she was left alone, although her morning-dress was perfect, and the lawn at Glene was a triumph of originally good turf and superior management. She could not take delight in such things when none were by to see her take delight in them. Accordingly she soon got up and sauntered into the house, and found Mr. Scorrier with her husband.

Rather than be by herself, she went into the room where they were. She was feeling so dull and discontented that she would have sought any society just then. Mr. Hepburn held his hand out to her, and smiled as she came in, and her face set itself more harshly than before. " This familiarity and kindness " to her before another man " was tasteless " she told herself, and then she tried to make herself believe that she did not care whether he thought it tasteless or not, and reminded herself that he was only the Danebury surgeon.

"I am just going down to have luncheon with Scorrier," Mr. Hepburn explained to her.

" Mr. Scorrier once asked me to go and see his conservatory," she said. A craving to go with them, not to be left alone, but to go and further disparage Cissy Vargrave in his eyes, if she could, seized her.

"I repeat my invitation for to-day, Mrs. Hepburn. Will you come and have luncheon in my den, too?" Mr. Scorrier said, with as much heartiness as his desire to be quit of her presence would permit him to infuse into his tone.

She was pondering something so deeply that she did not answer him immediately, and he, not liking her well enough to patiently wait her pleasure to speak, recommenced the conversation with Mr. Hepburn, which her appearance had interrupted. "So, as I was saying, I hope to be free early in next week for ten days or a fortnight."

"I will come, Mr. Scorrier. Thank you. I mean I shall be happy to come," Amelia interrupted, abruptly. "Where are you going to next week, did you say?"

"I did not say, but I will. I am going to Penzance, to stay with my mother."

A dark, angry flush suffused her face, and she glanced at him in the same sly, cautious way which has been already noticed. But she did not speak or take any other notice of his remarks.

"You won't stay for this affair at Castlenau, then, Arthur?" Mr. Hepburn asked.

"What affair?" Amelia said, quickly.

"Why, this dinner and ball. I almost think that, if I were in Arthur's place, I should go ; but I am old, and my dancing days are over, and I heartily wish I could avoid it."

"I did not tell Mr. Scorrier we would get him an invitation. I said I wished I could get him one," said Amelia, who much feared there was some mistake which might compromise her with the Countess in the matter.

"Oh! he has an invitation. Every one with a vote has, as a matter of course," Mr. Hepburn said, testily. And then Amelia went to prepare for her drive down to Danebury, to have luncheon with Mr. Scorrier.

She was feeling very sore and very much disgusted about several things. Amongst others, it was galling to find that when she came down with pomp and glory from her high estate, and expressed a loftily kind wish to do

him a great favour, that he should have had
the favour in his pocket the whole time. It
was not the least sharp part of the sting that
he should have had the magnanimity to strive
to spare her feelings by refraining from telling
her that this was the case. The tables were
turned upon her with a vengeance. She had
been trying to crush what he might deem
his claims to greater consideration than it was
her will and pleasure to accord him, by showing him in what high social esteem she was
held. And he had actually abstained from
putting the fact before her of himself being held
in equal esteem. She was deeply mortified,
and yet she could not hate and despise him
any more.

They all then drove down through the park
to the village in her pony-carriage. Amelia
was neither a skilful nor a graceful driver, but
her pair of bays and her little park phaeton
were alike perfect. She was never quite at ease
when she was guiding her spirited little steeds,
and the knowledge that she was not so, and
that she did not appear to be so, always dis-
composed her temper. Now, on this occasion,

she was feeling specially out of tune with her surroundings. Married woman as she was, *grande dame* as she believed herself to be, she was cut to the core at the thought of this young man, whom she had sneered at as a " country surgeon," having a higher feeling of admiration for Cecile Vargrave than for herself. Even with Glene and all its glories freshly in her mind, she could not help hoping, if this visit of his to Penzance boded what she feared, that his house might prove to be meanly proportioned and furnished. She could not help wishing that there might be something in its ordering and appointments which should cause mortification to Cecile, if ever the latter came there. And yet she could not hate and despise him any more.

They reached his house. Her husband had pointed out its garden-wall to her, on two or three occasions when they had been driving through Danebury, and she had looked at the same with the sort of tepid interest one is apt to feel for a place one does not know or care about.

But now she did look about her with interest,

as she passed through the gates and along the broad, sweeping, well-kept drive that led up to the entrance-door, which was shaded by a porch, covered in these August days with a thickly-starred jasmine and a wealth of cream-coloured roses. A long, two-storied house, verandahed and balconied into absolute beauty, with a number of large single-paned plate-glass windows gleaming out irregularly through masses of foliage and flowers. A pretty flat lawn in front, with a few shrubs and flower-beds on it. A limpid little sheet of water to the left, larger than a pond, smaller than a lake, with a reed-covered island about the size of a dining-table in it, and one dull but grace-ful swan floating on its breast. A conservatory to the right, running out from a door at the end of the house, through whose bright panes masses of rich colour, carefully grouped, could be seen. This was the exterior of Mr. Scorrier's house; and as Amelia looked about her, she could not help feeling that its tasteful, unpre-tentious beauty would be quite in keeping with Cissy Vargrave and Cissy Vargrave's ideas. "I could not bear to see her here," Mrs. Hep-

burn thought, compressing her cunning-looking,
rabbit-shaped mouth, as she walked through
the porch into the pretty entrance, which was
more ante-room than hall.

" Here, you see, in my drawing-room, I am
wanting in all those little ladylike uselessnesses
that speak of the feminine presence," Mr.
Scorrier said, throwing open a door, and usher-
ing his guests into a softly shaded, green-
tinted room, that if it was wanting in certain
" ladylike uselessnesses," certainly was wanting in little else. Those who are impatient of
upholstery details had better skip the remainder
of this page, for Mr. Scorrier's drawing-room,
as being closely illustrative of the man, de-
serves, and shall have, a full description. A
room, rather long and narrow, with a deep,
high bow-window at the further end ; panelled
walls in rather light, unvarnished, exquisitely
carved oak, and four light pillars of the same
(carved oak), springing from floor to ceiling,
and dividing the window-recess from the rest of
the room. A moss-patterned carpet, green and
brown, several low couches, all small, and easy
chairs of pomegranate-coloured velvet ; a piano

in oak-case ; a low, long oak book-case full of
splendidly bound volumes ; a velvet-covered
table (pomegranate-colour too), supported by a
shaft that sprang from the midst of a group of
lions shaped out of the same oak. These
things made up the furniture, the mere upholstery part of the room. But scattered about
in artistic confusion, were bronzes and sta-
tuettes in marble, mosaics, enamels, books, and
photographs.

"All this in Danebury!" Mrs. Hepburn
exclaimed, surprised into speech and out of
politeness.

CHAPTER VI.

A TRANSFORMATION.

"I WILL go and order luncheon," Mr. Scorrier said, as soon as he had brought his guests into this room. " Old Mrs. Wakely, my house-keeper, would be thrown out of gear by the thought of a lady at the table, if I didn't give her ten minutes' grace to make what she will think fitting alterations ;" then he went away, and Mr. and Mrs. Hepburn were free to do what people invariably do in an amusingly furnished room—namely, peer about, and criti-cising if they do not covet.

" His practice scarcely justifies all this, does it ? " Amelia said, when she had made the tour of inspection, seating herself as she spoke on one of the low couches, and trying to look round contemptuously. There was a curious

conflict of feeling going on within her. She
was not quite sure as to whether she felt more
pleased or aggrieved at this display of refine-
ment on the part of Mr. Scorrier, which he
had evidently not designed for her.

"Oh, I don't know," old Mr. Hepburn
replied; " he has private means."

"What made him settle down as a mere
surgeon?"

" My wish?"

"And why had you a wish on the subject of
the career of a young man who was no relation
to you?"

" I believe I have already told you why,
Amelia.   I knew his father."

"What is his mother like?" Amelia asked,
in a low tone.   But before Mr. Hepburn could
reply to this question, Arthur Scorrier came
back into the room.

"Now, Mrs. Hepburn," he said, "come, and
be indulgent to my bachelor entertainment,"
and then he offered her his arm and led her
into the dining-room.

" I am glad it is a bachelor entertainment,"
Mrs. Hepburn said, rather earnestly, as she

took her seat at the table, "at least," she added, in rather a confused tone, "one is glad of anything for a change, and it has always been my fate to be entertained by men's wives."

"Now, I was just thinking that a wife at the head of his table was the one grace wanting here," Mr. Hepburn said, looking about him approvingly. The table was round, and brightly set forth, and presently Mrs. Hepburn's attention was attracted by some old and richly chased little silver-gilt salt-cellars."

"These are lovely!" Amelia exclaimed. "Why, they are like ours, only smaller."

"They were my mother's contribution when I was putting my house in order," Arthur Scorrier said; "the only really valuable pieces of plate she had, I believe—my father's first present to her; had you noticed that they were the same pattern as yours, sir?" he added, addressing Mr. Hepburn.

"No, I had not," Mr. Hepburn replied, courteously; "singular coincidences of the kind are apt to occur about plate that was probably purchased about the same date. I see the crest has been obliterated."

"I suppose my father wanted to avoid paying tax for it," Arthur laughed. "By the way," he continued, "nothing of ours is marked with a crest. I don't know what mine is, Mrs. Hepburn. Isn't that a degrading confession, and are you not surprised at it?"

"No, I'm not surprised at it," Amelia said; but there was no covert sneer in her manner of saying it, as there would have been a short time ago. "Of course you could get it drawn from the heralds' office, if you liked."

"I should rather not do it, if I were in your place, Arthur," Mr. Hepburn said, advisingly. "Every young man who can get hold of a crest to which he has ever so remote a claim, sticks it on a signet-ring and a dog-cart, and whatever else he can conveniently place it on. I should prefer a simple cipher if I were in your place—it's better taste."

"But you can't call a son's claim to his father's crest a remote one," Amelia argued, and then felt sorry that she had spoken in favour of Mr. Scorrier's adopting an honourably distinctive badge, which she should sorely grudge to Cissy Vargrave's husband. "If I felt sure that he would marry her, I would suggest his adopting a pill-box even now," she thought, savagely; and then she looked at his frank, high-spirited, handsome face, and marked his look of breeding, and felt regretful for the savage desire to snub him which had seized her but a moment before. "But if he goes hankering after a wife whose connections or want of connections will only lower him socially, he will deserve any amount of snubbing," she told herself.

By-and-by the conversation turned to the seasonable topic of travelling.

"It's so natural, after having lived all my life in London, to think that it's absolutely necessary to go somewhere else in the autumn," Mrs. Hepburn said. "I have the feeling on me now, though, of course, I couldn't have fresher air or lovelier scenery anywhere than at Glene."

"Yes, you have plenty of fresh air and good scenery here, but it's inland air and scenery, and what one wants in autumn are sea-breezes and coast-scenery. Why don't you go down to Penzance now your friends are there?" Arthur

Scorrier asked, forgetting, in his eagerness to secure a means of communion with Cecile Vargrave, that his mother's presence would be a barrier to Mr. Hepburn's helping him.

"Because I saw quite enough of my friends, as you persist in calling them, when I was living near them," Amelia said, coldly.

"And I may add, because I have an insurmountable objection to Penzance," her husband added, with equal coldness. Then the spirit of quiet enjoyment and geniality which had been about this trio before, fled, and they each felt that the sooner they separated the pleasanter it would be for all.

They went back to the drawing-room that was so striking in its oak-panelled unconventionality, and when Mrs. Hepburn was sitting waiting for her ponies to come round, Mr. Scorrier came up to her, and addressed her with greater heartiness than he had ever expressed towards her before.

"You will come again—this first visit will not be your last?"

She looked up half sullenly, half smilingly. "Why should I come again? You only ask me because you want my husband, and ho would come without me."

"I must not have you leave with that impression; it is too mortifying to me; you make me feel that I have been signally wanting in one of the finer attributes of hospitality—what have I done?"

"You have not done anything yet," sho said; and it was all sullenness now—sullenness unredeemed by an attempt at a smile.

" What is he likely to do that can be displeasing to you, my dear?" Mr. Hepburn asked, speaking sharply, and looking sharply at them both; and then Amelia threw off the sombre cloud that had settled over her with an effort, and rose up laughing.

" Why, if he married a Miss Pottinger, for instance, I could not help being displeased, I should never have the courage to come here and bore myself."

"I shall never marry a Miss Pottinger," Arthur Scorrier replied, as he offered his arm, and led her out to her pony-carriage. "Meantime, until I commit a similar iniquity, let there be peace and good-will between us."

He spoke lightly, in the merest jest. But there was sober earnest in her tone as she answered,

"So be it—until you commit a similar iniquity, as you say." Then the old husband and the hard young wife drove off together, and as Mr. Scorrier watched them through his gates, he thought,

"We shall both regret the day he married the blameless creature whose name was never even whispered in connection with a girlish flirtation. She either wants to play a dangerous game, or she is conjuring up a more dangerous reality." And then he went about his work again, disliking his old friend's wife more in this first hour of her partially relenting towards him, than he had ever done while she had been half insolently opposed to him.

"As we are in the village, I should like to call in and see Mrs. Pottinger," Mr. Hepburn said, breaking a silence which had lasted from the time they had exchanged "good-bye" with Arthur Scorrier.

"As you please," Mrs. Hepburn replied,

quickly. "I was thinking myself that it was time that I went to see her."

There was something so unusually acquiescent in Amelia's voice and manner that Mr. Hepburn looked at her in surprise, telling himself that it must have been the concession he had made in the matter of Castlenau which had wrought the happy change. He thought he would improve the occasion.

"I don't care at all for society, as you know," he said, in a tone that showed how eminently praiseworthy and commendable he thought such "not caring" was, "still, I like to see old friends about me in my own house. I wish you would sometimes ask those girls up of an evening to have coffee and a little music."

"Girls find coffee and a little music dull without anything else; but if they will find any pleasure in coming, I shall be very happy to see them."

Another concession! Amelia had not been so amiably ready to fall in with his views since their marriage.

"You could always ask Scorrier to come in,

too," he said, as they turned down the little side-road in which Mrs. Pottinger's was situated; and Amelia, still affable, answered, "Yes, he is good-natured enough not to mind trying to help amuse the poor old things."

This was only the second time that Mrs. Hepburn of Glene had condescended from her high estate so far as to call on Mrs. Pottinger. She had often pulled her ponies up at the widow's door, and left baskets of vegetables, and fruit, and flowers, but in her narrow fear of getting intimate with wrong people, and so damaging herself in the county, she had never " gone in " after making the compulsory return call on just coming to Glene. As she went in this day there was an odour of dried lavender and pot-pourri, of old-fashioned stocks and jasmine, and a great air of respectability and quiet that made her wish for a moment that she could "feel like it," feel settled, feel satisfied and contented—as was her husband, for instance. They went into a comfortably furnished, faded, chintz-covered room, where the odour of dried lavender and pot-pourri strengthened, and there they found the widow, Mrs. Pottinger, and her four unmarried daughters doing the work that was established in their minds by habit and custom as the "right kind of work to do of an afternoon." This was wool-work, all stiff in design and sad in colour, copied from much pricked and worn patterns of forty years ago—patterns that were kept alive, so to say, by much brown paper and gum at their backs, and that would never gratify the vulgar gaze even when finished. For it was a fixed and immutable law in Mrs. Pottinger's house that everything which, in the distorted imaginations of the dwellers therein ranked as pretty, should be covered up religiously under large and grotesque-patterned chintzes.

"And so you really have been to luncheon at Mr. Scorrier's!" Mrs. Pottinger began, as soon as her guests were seated. Mrs. Pottinger was a slim, tight-figured old lady, with cleanly-cut aquiline features, that were now becoming beaky—an old lady who spoke in a flat monotone, and who prided herself still on the possession of a waist. She was likewise much addicted to the pleasure of telling people what they had been doing lately, without waiting to know whether such show of knowledge on her part would be agreeable to them or not. An old lady who took an active interest in her fellow-creatures still, an interest which would lead her to get out of bed at unseemly hours, and peer through the blinds to see when and how her neighbours came home from market and other places. This habit of hers had driven her only married daughter and son-in-law out of Danebury, for, as her daughter said, "It is too much to do an uninteresting thing one hour, and to be told of it by mamma the next."

" And so you really have been to luncheon at Mr. Scorrier's !" she began, to which remark Amelia smiled a faint assent, and Mr. Hepburn replied, heartily:

" Yes, it has been my wife's first visit there, and Arthur entertained us well. Did he not, Amelia?"

" Very well indeed," Mrs. Hepburn said, carelessly. She did not wish to discuss either Mr. Scorrier or Mr. Scorrier's *ménage* just yet.

" He is a very superior young man, don't you think?" Mrs. Pottinger went on; and Amelia asked impertinently :

" Superior to what ?—his position and the people he lives amongst ? Yes, I think he is."

" I mean superior to most young men of the day," Mrs. Pottinger, who evidently declined to feel rebuffed, replied: " his house is too fantastic for my taste, but he has travelled a great deal, and picked up queer notions that don't quite fall in with our ideas."

" I thought his house very perfect," Amelia said, steadily; " it didn't strike me as being fantastic at all."

" Didn't it, really! Well, as I said to his mother, when she was staying with him, and she agreed with me—most excellent and delightful person, his mother—I was quite sorry you were not here, Mr. Hepburn, to make her acquaintance, you would have been charmed with her—I told her so, and added that she would have been delighted with you, and she said she hoped to meet you some day."

" Don't you know his mother?" Amelia asked, quite disregarding the fact of the latter part of Mrs. Pottinger's speech being merely a long parenthetical interruption to the statement she was about to make, relative to the same sentiments being held in common on a certain subject by both Mrs. Scorrier and herself, "Don't you know his mother?"

"No, I do not," Mr. Hepburn replied, testily. It was very disagreeable to him to hear remarks made about that fine avoidance of Mrs. Scorrier which he had explained so satisfactorily to her son.

"We used to see a great deal of her while she was here," one of the Misses Pottinger struck in; "she was always asking us there, so different from some mothers, who are afraid if a girl looks at their sons." Miss Pottinger quite flushed up in excitement as she said this, and Mrs. Hepburn regarded her with a gaze that said only too plainly, "No mother need be afraid of you."

"Yes, it would be very nice for us if Mrs. Scorrier came to live with her son," a second Miss Pottinger said, enthusiastically; "she paid us so very much attention that we missed her very much when she left. I do wonder that Mr. Scorrier does not have her with him; he is not likely to marry, I should think."

"There is no one for him to marry about

here," Amelia said, contemptuously, disregarding ruthlessly the claims to his consideration which the Misses Pottinger might be supposed to have by lenient and easily satisfied people; and then, being away from the influence of his presence, she went on to give utterance to one of the views respecting him with which she had fortified her dislike to him at first. " Mr. Scorrier can't afford to marry anybody; men in his position have need to marry wives who can help them up."

"I think you will find that Mr. Scorrier, when he does marry, will do so to please himself, without much regard to other people's thoughts on the subject," Mr. Hepburn said, energetically. " I hope he will marry well and happily, and soon—above all, soon; I should like to see him with a wife in his youth."

" I have no doubt he will gratify you, if you only let him know your wishes on the subject," Amelia said, suffering her temper to rise, but keeping it in check, because she would not let the Pottingers think that all was not bliss in this marriage of hers; " for my own part, I can't understand taking a wild interest in a

man's marriage before there is the faintest probability of his marrying at all.　Can you?"

"No, I can't," Mrs. Pottinger said, promptly,
actuated by the amiable desire of agreeing with
both Mr. Hepburn and his wife; "but then,
you see, a Mrs. Scorrier would be rather an
important person in our village society.　We
naturally feel that a good many of our little
social pleasures would be made or marred by
her, so we can't help questioning what she
might be like."

"A bright fate for anybody, that, certainly!
Humdrum and monotonous as my life is, Cissy
Vargrave will find hers more insignificant still
if he is fool enough to marry her," Amelia
thought.　And then she put on the appearance
of listening politely .to some of the Pottinger
platitudes, while in reality she was indulging
herself in the reflection that if such a marriage
should come to pass, Cissy's excitable, impatient,
discontented nature would wear itself out in the
ignominious bondage it would be placed in, between the neglects of some and the attentions
of others.

The good temper and easy acquiescence in

any suggestions he made, which had so surprised and pleased Mr. Hepburn half an hour before, were quite gone now. She looked as she felt, weary, cross, and worn-out, as she sat there and thought, this then was all her marriage had brought her. This! that she should spend her young life in a humdrum, monotonous way, and be made by circumstances to find her keenest interest and greatest pleasure in the hope that her old friend Cissy Vargrave might know nothing brighter. Then she angrily checked these thoughts, trying to drive them out, and crush them down, by telling herself that, after all, she had no reason for supposing that Cissy would ever be nearer and dearer to this young man than she was at present. Even if Arthur Scorrier did go to Penzance, a thousand things might occur, and probably would occur, to prevent his meeting with the Vargraves. Besides, something might stop his going to Penzance. She rose up to go away, giving the Pottingers a far warmer invitation to "come and spend the evening at Glene," in her haste, than she would have accorded them had she felt cool and collected as usual. She

would go home and send a verbal invitation to
Mr. Scorrier to come to them this evening,
" for the sake of amusing the poor, dull, prosy
Pottingers ;" and if he came, she would say
just one or two little words to him about the
Vargraves that should show him what she
thought of them. She was quite absorbed in
these determinations as she drove home—quite
absorbed in the work of proving to herself that
the sudden desire to entertain these people was
due, solely and wholly to the fact of her having
discovered that the sight of any one at Glene,
was better than the solitude she had recently
endured. And that the other resolve, the in_
tention of saving Mr. Scorrier, at any cost, from
the Vargrave snare, was due to the fact of his
being such a favourite of her husband's. " I
will find out what his mother is like, and get her
on my——" she checked the reflection, and
changed it into the words, " and get her to
regard it as a *mésalliance*." For somehow or
other Amelia had learnt that the fear of her son
making one was one of the strongest and most
painful feelings in the old lady's mind. How
she had arrived at this knowledge of the senti-

ments of the old lady, mention of whom was so
rarely made, it is hard to say. But she had
arrived at it. She felt that it was so, and
for some reason or other she was very glad
of it.

It was well for their married happiness perhaps that she had something to think about on
this occasion, which carried her outside Mr.
Hepburn's influence, as it were. For Mr.
Hepburn's influence would have been a depressing one had she been sympathetic to it: an annoying one had she been unsympathetic and, at
the same time, observant. On the face of it
she had been very conceding in act and deed (if
not in manner always) this day, and it was, or
rather it would have been, had she observed it,
hard to find these acts and deeds disregarded,
or regarded as trifles now. She had accepted
the invitation of his favourite, and she had extended invitations to his friends the Pottingers,
and this was a great move in the conciliating
direction away from her resolution to have "Nothing at all to do with them," with which she
had been fraught when she first came to Glene.
But Mr. Hepburn was evidently ill-pleased about

something. Whether it was with her or with
another, it was difficult to determine. He
showed his displeasure as they drove home by
maintaining a grim silence, and a rigid expression of face; and of these signs of displeasure Amelia took no notice. When he
reached home, he manifested it more openly.

" I thought it in very bad taste your talking
as you did about Mrs. Scorrier, Amelia," he
said, in a vexed tone.

" Talking as I did about Mrs. Scorrier! I
scarcely mentioned her," Amelia said, and then
she added, quickly; "Your friends, the Misses
Pottinger made themselves geese about her;
but that they do about every one they mention."

" Arthur is surely the best judge of whether
it would be agreeable to have his mother live
with him or not," Mr. Hepburn went on, just
as though the scheme of Mrs. Scorrier's doing
so had been started by Amelia.

" I think it would be a hateful plan for him
to have her there," Mrs. Hepburn answered,
with considerable energy. " It's one of those
houses that are pleasant enough to go to as

we went to-day, but that would be odious with a mistress in it."

" Not with a wife for its mistress. We shall have him there with a wife soon, I hope," Mr. Hepburn replied; and then he went on, " I look forward to seeing him settled in the best way a man can be settled before I die."

"I think," Amelia said, rising up slowly (she had seated herself to listen to Mr. Hepburn's views respecting Arthur Scorrier's settling)—" I think I had better go and dress for dinner now."

" You will be too early; come out on the lawn with me."

"As you please; but I am very tired." Then she made a step forward after him towards the door, and he heard her stagger, catch hold of a light chair that turned over in her grasp, and looked round in time to see her falling to the ground quite cold and insensible.

He was only lately married, and his hopes as to what might eventuate from his marriage were high, consequently he was very much frightened now at what looked very like physi-

cal delicacy in his wife. She had not been
having too much excitement since her marriage,
he had taken care of that, and this day she
had been subjected to the test of only the
gentlest driving exercise. He was shocked and
disappointed and frightened. She had always
seemed to be so sound and hard and hearty ;
so entirely free from all that over-sensitiveness
of mind and body to which some feminine
flesh is heir. This sudden failing of that
sound, hard heartiness, on which he had so
strongly relied, upset him very much. In a
minute, as he stood looking at her crumpled
up on the carpet at his feet, he thought of all
the restoratives of which he had heard—water,
burnt feathers, toilet vinegar, a doctor! The
last was likely to prove the most efficacious.
He rang the bell, and when the servant came
in, he ordered that a messenger might be des-
patched, desiring Mr. Scorrier's immediate
attendance on Mrs. Hepburn, and then he sat
down and watched her as she gradually panted
back to consciousness.

"What is it that has upset you so," he
asked, as she recovered, and sat up, looking

very white and stricken still, as he had never seen her look before.

" Nothing—I turned giddy," she said, and then she stood up and muttered something about " now she would go and dress."

" Wait here, Amelia ; I have sent for Scorrier ; do wait here, and see him, my dear."

" Sent for Scorrier !" she said, sharply ; " what utter absurdity !"

"My intense anxiety about you was the cause of the absurdity," he replied, in rather an injured tone. " I wanted to know what was the matter with you. The attack has shaken me more than it has you, Amelia," he added, tenderly ; " it will be a satisfaction to me for Scorrier to see you."

" It will be no satisfaction to me, but only a great annoyance," she said, retreating towards the door. And then he resumed authority, told her that " this was mere senseless prejudice," and then was left alone—till Mr. Scorrier came—to ruminate on the probabilities of his wife proving contumacious.

She went upstairs, and went through the

ceremony of dressing with an impatient anxiety
that did not escape the eyes of her maid. Apparently, Mrs. Hepburn was more desirous of
setting off such natural charms as she was
possessed of, with all the artifices of art she
had at her command this day, than she had
been since her marriage.   Usually when they
were alone—and they were always alone at
Glene—she was content with whatever dress
the taste of Olive, her maid, condemned her
to wear.   But this day she took the selection
into her own hands, and routed all Olive's
suggestions.   Hitherto the handsome young
wife of the old master of Glene had seemed to
affect sombre colours, and matronly forms in
her attire—putting ten years on to herself, if
she put a day, by such reckless indiscretion in
the choice of dress, as Olive was wont to aver.
But now some change was wrought ·in her
judgment respecting what it would be fit and
proper for her to wear, to sit down to dine
alone with Mr. Hepburn in.   At length she
stood arrayed in a soft, filmy Indian muslin,
about which a trellis-work of the most exquisitely delicate embroidery seemed to creep—

a robe so soft and transparent that it only
veiled and did not dim the brightly blue crys-
talline silk, over which it fell—when at length
she stood arrayed thus, it was evident that her
youth and good looks were going to assert
themselves in a way she had never encouraged
them to do before. Then she sent down to
the conservatory for some crimson flowers, and
placed them in her hair and on her bosom;
and then she decked her hard, white, thin,
well-formed hands, with sparkling rings, and
looked at herself in the glass, and was pleased.

In the glass, too, besides the reflection of
her own good looks, so well set off, she caught
the face of her maid set in a stare of amaze-
ment and amusement. It was not her policy
at all (if policy she had) to turn round and
detect, and force an explanation from the
shrewd waiting-woman. But she determined
to do away with both these feelings in Olive's
mind—these feelings which were so vividly
portrayed in Olive's face. Accordingly she
waited, in apparent unconsciousness, for a
minute or two, fashioning and refashioning the
disposition of her flowers. And then her

cunning eyes (they were cunning in spite of
being well-formed and good in colour, and altogether what people generally called fine) raised
themselves, and she turned round.

" Mr. Hepburn is more particular about the
way in which I dress to receive such old and
valued friends as Mrs. Pottinger and her
daughters, than if I were dressing for a ball,"
she said; and Olive thought, " Mr. Hepburn
can never think to please them old things by
getting her to look like their granddaughter."

CHAPTER VII.

MRS. HEPBURN'S WEAKNESS.

MR. SCORRIER had obeyed the summons to Glene without delay. Amelia had barely put the finishing stroke to her preparations for the gratification of the pride of the eye in the Pottingers, by quelling all conjecture in her maid, before there came a knock at her dressing-room door; and she was told that Mr. Scorrier had arrived.

"I don't want the doctor here; you can tell Mr. Hepburn that I will come down," she said; and then she hastily gathered up her arms—her fan and all the paraphernalia of female warfare—and went down stairs to submit to an investigation into her state of health. Mr. Hepburn met her in the hall, and began a reproof of her imprudence in "having exerted

herself so far, when Scorrier could just as well
have gone up to her." But she smiled so
deprecatingly in acknowledgment of this reproof, and seemed altogether so very much
softened by the effects of that faint, feminine
lapse out of herself of which she had been
guilty, that he tried to turn the reproof into a
caress, which she could not bear after all she
had gone through this day. She put his arm
down, away from her quickly, and went on
hurriedly into the drawing-room, apologizing
for her action as she went.

"A straw would knock me down just now—
it would, indeed, Mr. Hepburn; it's the first
time in my life that my nerves have given
way, and I can't recover directly." With these
words she came into Mr. Scorrier's presence,
beautifully dressed, flushed from some cause—
weakness perhaps—with a flush he had never
seen in her face before, a little agitated, and
very much altered.

But not more altered than he was. She had
seen him last gay and lively, or at least as gay
and lively as it is possible for a man to be when
there is no special call made on these qualities;

and now he met her stiffly and gravely and professionally, in a way that made her very much wish that she had not fainted, or that her husband had not sent for Mr. Scorrier towards her restoration.

"I turned giddy—it was sudden and complete prostration; I am not very strong, and I suppose I had been over-fatigued this morning," she said, in reply to his inquiries. Then she placed herself in a chair, with her back to the light, and began fanning herself vigorously, hoping the kindly shade would conceal the unusual brightness of her eyes and burning of her cheeks.

"There is no sign of weakness, or of anything but the most perfect health in that," he said, when he had felt her pulse.

"I knew it; I did not wish you to be sent for; but now that you are here, I may be spared writing a note which Mr. Hepburn would have had me write otherwise. Come to us at eight to-night, will you?—the Pottingers are coming."

"I am afraid I am not free to-night," he said.

"So many engagements in Danebury! really I beg your pardon for having given you such an unceremonious invitation."

She spoke bitterly now; the evening did loom so long and heavily before her.

"It's no pleasure engagement, it's a business engagement, Mrs. Hepburn." Then he turned to Mr. Hepburn and assured him that there was no need for anxiety. "Every sign of Mrs. Hepburn's indisposition has passed;" and then the dinner-bell warned him to depart.

Mr. Hepburn went out as far as the hall-door with him, questioning him anxiously as they went.

"You said that to reassure her, Arthur," he said, earnestly; "but tell me the truth—it would be a terrible thing for me to lose her, or to see her suffer."

"Mrs. Hepburn is as sound in health as a roach, sir;" Arthur Scorrier replied; "perhaps change of air and scene would strengthen her though, and keep her in as sound health as she is now."

"But I have always considered Glene the healthiest place in England. We stand on a height; we get the breeze that blows straight away from the Devonshire moors down that line of valley ; and the drainage is perfect."

"Still Glene may not suit Mrs. Hepburn's constitution. However, dinner is the object in hand with you now," he added, laughing; "you can think about when it would be well to travel by-and-by." Then he went away, leaving Mr. Hepburn rather ill-pleased with him for not taking a deeper and more intense interest in Amelia's health.

"You gave me a terrible turn, my dear—thank heaven it is no worse than it is!" Mr. Hepburn said to his wife, watching her with a sort of observant fondness that she felt it was hard to have to endure "at her age." She was constantly remembering her age now, and contrasting it with his ; and this, not because she wished to do it, but because she could not help doing it.

"No worse than it is! I told you it was nothing, and Mr. Scorrier told you the same thing, which, by the way, was not too polite of him," she said. Then they went in to dinner, as they had gone in to dinner every day since she first came to Glene, and were served, with comfort and orderly celerity, to a dinner that was as unexceptionable as were all the dinners at Glene. But the edge of her appetite was taken off; perhaps it was by the reflection that the evening would be very long, and that the Pottingers were coming.

" Arthur advises change of air and scene for you, my dear," Mr. Hepburn said, with a little gulp, as soon as the servants left the room. " I must find out where you wish to go, and when it would be well for you to go."

" You would not leave Glene ! " she cried ; and she looked aghast at the proposition that was made so entirely for her good.

" I would not leave it for any lighter consideration. But your health is everything."

" What nonsense this is ! " she said, angrily. " My health ! What does Mr. Scorrier mean by pronouncing me robust one instant, and counselling change of air and scene for the good of my health the next ? "

" I thought," Mr. Hepburn began, and then he paused, and seemed to be considering whether it would be advisable for him to finish the sentence he had commenced or not.

"You thought I valued your comfort less highly than I do, when you believed that I would consent to a plan that would be anything but a pleasure to you," she said, in a low voice. "I shall be distressed—really I shall—if you say any more about taking me away; my health does not need it, and I am getting fond of Glene."

Then they heard that Mrs. and the Misses Pottinger had arrived, and Amelia rose up hastily.

"We must not let them feel they are too soon," she said, in explanation of her hasty movement, as she passed Mr. Hepburn at the door; and he could not help thinking how very much more amiable she had become this day, though to think so was treason against what she had been before.

Evidently the Pottingers had come anticipating a sort of little gala. Justifiably so; for had not Mrs. Hepburn said that she should ask Mr. Scorrier to meet them? and with Mr. Scorrier for a fellow-guest, and Mr. and Mrs.

Hepburn for their host and hostess, a gala it would have been.

But now, by reason of the absence of Mr. Scorrier, the festival was robbed of half its festivity, in the eyes of the younger ladies. The Misses Pottinger were all past that age when prettiness is easily attainable; that age when the hair asserts itself as a silky and luxuriant fact, no matter how badly arranged it is, and the quick bloom of youth will mount to the cheek, however slight the encouragement it may receive to do so. They were compelled to be very painstaking now in the matter of their toilet, when they desired to create a favourable impression. That they had taken such pains to-night was palpable. Mrs. Hepburn almost felt pityingly towards them as she thought of the circumspection with which they must have moved and had their being, from the moment they had inducted themselves into the creaseless, starchy muslins in which they now appeared.

"We were quite alarmed about you," Mrs. Pottinger said, as Amelia went forward to meet her, and Mrs. Pottinger's face assumed an appearance of the deepest and most intense anxiety. "We saw the groom pass at a full gallop, and then pull up at Mr. Scorrier's door, and I said to Fanny, 'Depend upon it, that's no· invitation, carried at such a pace— dear Mrs. Hepburn is ill!' It was quite a relief to us all when we saw Mr. Scorrier come back, and we asked him how you were, and he spoke of it as a slight attack."

"It was nothing at all—it wasn't worthy the name of 'an attack,'" Amelia said, decidedly. " I felt faint, or sick, or giddy, or something, and Mr. Hepburn made un unnecessary fuss about it, very much to my annoyance."

"Mr. Scorrier tells us he has recommended change for you," Fanny Pottinger said, eagerly ; " so unkind of him not to think of something else that would strengthen you ! What would Glene be like if you left now ? "

"Does Mr.· Scorrier think me weak ?" Amelia asked, tartly, disregarding the flattery.

" Yes ; he said he thought it was weakness."

"I shall be stronger by-and-by, under his advice," said Mrs. Hepburn ; and then she moved to the piano and opened it, and sug-

gested that one of the Misses Pottinger should
play something—" for we must make the best
of each other to-night ; " she explained. " Mr.
Scorrier had a business engagement, and could
not come, and everyone else we know lives a
hundred miles off." Then, when they heard
that Mr. Scorrier had a business engagement,
they felt that their circumspection in the matter
of the muslins had been vain, and that there
would be no gala at Glene that evening.

It was a hard, long evening for Amelia, and
indeed it is difficult to see in what way one bit
of the hard length of it could have been ob-
viated. The sweetest amiability and the most
intense desire on her part to please, would
scarcely have wrought a beneficial change in
the social atmosphere. They had no interests,
no hopes, no memories in common. Mrs.
Pottinger's experience of the world was limited.
Before her marriage she had been a governess
in a midland county clergyman's family. From
thence she had moved to a western county, and
become the wife of another clergyman. She
had always been admirable in her family and
exemplary in the parish. She was good, but

she was dull, with a deep, satisfied, good-tempered dulness that was a dreary thing to endure. Her daughters were cut after the same pattern as herself, with an even more limited experience, for they had never migrated from Danebury. Amelia felt all her usual topics of conversation were cut from beneath her feet as she talked with these women, and knew that, if she touched on anything beyond local gossip, it would merely lead them into a conversational *cul de sac* from whence there would be no escape.

She almost envied the facility with which her husband talked, and led them to talk in return. Not that the words of either led to much, but they passed away the time, and that was something, since the time had to be passed away. She was not a clever woman or a brilliant woman, but she was used to the flash, and glitter, and ever-changing aspect of London life, and a great greyness clouded her horizon. Now that she was brought into the leafy wilderness, and offered no excitement in the place of that flash and glitter, she began to recognize a great truth. She had stultified the feelings of

youth within her breast while they were hers to
indulge freely. They were not hers to indulge
freely any more, and they now would assert
themselves, and struggle to have fair play.
" The worst that will ever happen to me will
be having to bear a horrible heart-ache," she
thought, with painful prescience ; " and I'm
strong enough to bear that in silence."

What a long, hard evening, unredeemed by
any prospect of anything a shade brighter !
She looked at the group assembled in that
drawing-room as it was reflected in the large
glass at the end of the room—looked at it as
though it had been a picture, and pondered
over it. In the foreground she saw herself, a
girl still—a hard-faced and sad one—but only
a girl, with long, long years before her to live,
in the nature of things, and a vow upon her
always to live to herself, unloved and unloving.
Then she glanced at " the girls,"—as their
mother called them still—the girls whose girlhood was so venerable in comparison with her
own, and remembered that they were the
children of the old lady in the background,
who looked a fitting mate for the old gentle-

man with whom she (the old lady) was growing
so garrulous! She could not help feeling that,
if Mr. Scorrier had come, she would not have
had so much time to draw comparisons that
were hateful to her. She could not help re-
membering that he was chiefly anxious to fulfil
his business engagement, in order that he
might be able to get away to Cecile Vargrave's
presence.

"I could bear to have her living there, so
near to me, if he had been different," she
thought; though in what she would have
wished him to be different it was hard to say.
But at any rate the thought of him as he was,
and the thought of Cecile and where she might
eventually be, irritated Amelia almost beyond
all power of patiently enduring the society
which she had brought upon herself this
night.

If she had only been able to go on looking
down upon this young Danebury surgeon; if
she had only been able to go on distrusting
her own prudence in holding intimate communion—the intimate communion which her
husband seemed to desire—with this mere

parish professional; if she had only been strong enough to hold to her first intention of keeping him in the second place always, she would not have grudged the position of his wife to Cissy Vargrave. But she had not been able to do any of these things, and so she did grudge that position to Cissy, who had never succumbed to her in the old days of girlish intercourse and rivalries (all unconnected with the heart) at Bayswater.

It is a difficult thing to decide what made Mrs. Hepburn remember this night that she had never been in love. But the memory of this truth did cross her mind, and she could not shake it off. She had always been watchful and wary over her affections, not suffering them to stray into forbidden or dubious paths. She had always conducted herself in a cool and exemplary manner at balls and pic-nics, in opera boxes, and in running the gauntlet of the morning promenade and afternoon drives in the Park. No man had ever pressed her hand, or looked into her eyes lovingly, or won loving looks from her. She had always been cool and collected, and her course of conduct had an-

swered admirably. Had she not married
young and well? What other girl of that
Bayswater coterie to which she belonged had
married a man whose ancestor had entertained
Queen Elizabeth, and who had, at the same
time, been fortunate enough to have in his possession the very mansion in which such entertainment had taken place? But, on the other
hand, what good did this glorious fact do her?
She never saw any one to whom she could tell
it, and it was an honour and glory that, gloated
over in private only, was very apt to pall.

She was roused from these reflections by the
fluttering towards her of Mrs. Pottinger, and
gathering her faculties together, she was enabled to understand that some question had
been asked her which was of great importance
to the others, and which had fallen unmean-
ingly on her ears.

"I say that, of course, you'll be too happy,"
Mr. Hepburn was saying; "but Mrs. Pottinger
will have the assurance from your own lips."

"What is it?" Amelia asked.

"Why, it's about this ball at Castlenau,"
Mrs. Pottinger began, explainingly. "An invi-

tation has come for us,—for me and two of
the girls,—through the interest of my brother-
in-law, Mr. Pottinger—the lawyer, you know,
who is Mr. Walter Bracey's solicitor.   Oh ! you
will be delighted with Mr. Pottinger, Mrs.
Hepburn; such a head he has; it's wonderful,
as I often say, where he keeps all the subjects
his brain is busy upon; such a deep mind, and
such judgment; you will appreciate him, but
the world generally does not know what he
is."

"But about this ball?" Amelia asked, impatiently.

"That is what I am coming to.   Mr. Pottinger, with his customary kindness, and in the
midst of his own enormous responsibilities, is
always thinking if he can do his nieces a kindness.   So now he has procured us this invitation; and as, for many reasons, I don't care to
go, I am anxious to find some one who will be
kind enough to take them.   Mr. Hepburn says
you will be so kind; but I cannot think of im-
posing on you so far; I could not, indeed."

The vision of splendour and county consideration which the invitation to Castlenau had

conjured up, was pretty well broken already. But as Mrs. Pottinger spoke it was utterly shattered and destroyed—this, that she had deemed an honour and a privilege, was shared apparently by every obscure person in the region round about!

"They may just as well go with us," was all she could bring herself to say. And then, although it was growing late, Mrs. Pottinger would grow ecstatic, and stay to consult the beneficent lady of Glene as to what dresses the girls should wear.

"As if it mattered how a lot of old maids arrayed themselves!" Amelia thought, angrily, when the Pottingers were at last on their way home in a Glene carriage. "What a first appearance it will be for me to make, to be sure!" This was the sort of thing, then, for which she had sacrificed her youth, and the youthful power and happiness of loving well—this, that she should chaperone about a lot of middle-aged women, who would not add to her pleasure, or her prestige, in any way. Her heart was dull and heavy that night as she put off the filmy muslin and the crimson flowers. Better to have been the mistress of some meaner place than Glene, and to have known a little of the joy of early mistress-ship, than to be closed in as she was on every side from every gratification which she had led herself to believe she should have. Even her pleasure in the coming ball at Castlenau was tarnished now, and yet again, after that ball there would be nothing. She felt that if she did go to bed she could not sleep. So she sat down and commenced a long letter to Cissy Vargrave. It is so natural to turn to a friend, or on an enemy, in time of inner troubles. Her letter to my heroine shall be transcribed, as it will help to a clearer understanding of what is to come :—

"My dear Cissy,—I have been waiting impatiently for another letter from Isabelle, giving me some more satisfactory address than 'Post Office, Penzance.' I want to hear that you are settled at some charming hotel, looking on to the Esplanade, where we can come and join you shortly. Glene is so unhealthy now that my medical attendant has ordered change of air for me; therefore, it is out of

the question that I should try to beguile you
away from the fresh sea-air, as I had hoped
and intended to do. If my health obliges me
to remain away from Glene for any length of
time, I believe I shall actually fret. Brief as
my experience of my new home has been, I
am devoted to it—as, indeed, any one with the
smallest taste for the beautiful, old, and interesting, must be. It is something to have
married into a family that has been powerful
and considerable for so many generations as
the Hepburns have been. The only drawbacks
to the most perfect enjoyment here are the
great distances between ourselves and the only
friends we can have in the county, such as the
Castlenau people, &c.; for it would be pride
aping humility, indeed, if we were to pretend
to be on terms of equality with the village re-
spectabilities about us. However, I am not
put to any pain or annoyance by this, as none
of the excellent doctresses and lawyeresses expect to be made uncomfortable by invitations
to Glene. Do you remember Lady Ellington
and her daughters, Lady Clara and Lady Au-
drey, holding a stall at a bazaar for the benefit

of poor governesses once? How she will laugh
when she sees the moveable monkey pen-wiper
I bought that day! Write and tell me your
plans soon, as it may be that I shall have to
make up my mind quickly as to where I shall
go for change of air. I should battle on at
Glene (it is so hard to leave a magnificent place
that is your own, for more or less uncomfortable lodgings), but I have not the heart to disregard my husband's anxiety about me. Do
let me know about your stay at Penzance—not
that I am likely to be able to join you there;
and do believe that at some future time I shall
be delighted to welcome you at Glene. I suppose things go on much as usual in the dusty,
glaring squares, of which you must be even
more heartily tired than I am, seeing that you
have lived more grown-up years in them. Do
you know anything of Mr. Scorrier's mother?—
she lives at Penzance.

　　　　　" Your affectionate friend,
　　　　　　　　" AMELIA HEPBURN."

This letter was received by Cecile Vargrave
one morning, just after she had been bathing,

and had come in to breakfast in very good fresh spirits. With an utter disregard, or forgetfulness for once, of the sacredness of correspondence, she claimed attention from all at the table, and almost asked for their comments upon it, by saying, when she had brought her reading to a close, "Isn't that a delicious effusion, and uncommonly like Amelia?"

"It's very delightful to hear from her herself that she is so happy," Mrs. Vargrave said, warmly.

"And it's very delightful, as we most likely shall stay there some day or other, to hear that Glene is such a charming place," Isabelle added.

"And it's most touching to hear her tribute to her husband's anxiety about her health," Mr. Vargrave put in, laughing.

"But the most delightful and touching sentence in the letter is the gratifying acknowledgment she makes of my well-established seniority," Cissy said, with a smile that would have been brighter had she not been a woman wincing under the vengeful mention of something that another woman deemed less than pleasant.

"I am sure Amelia could never have thought you would care for that, my dear," Mrs. Vargrave said, with a large air of explanation. "It is only weak-minded women, who wish to seem younger than they are, who are sensitive about their age. Amelia knows you too well, and thinks too highly of your good sense, to speak of you being a little older than herself in a slighting way; and it's very pretty of her to speak in that way about being willing to go away to please her husband, though she is so fond of her own home—very pretty indeed."

"Very," Cissy answered; "I'm going to write and tell her so."

"If you do write to-day, give her my love, and tell her that I hope we shall see her here, if only that I may carry back a favourable report to her mother about her," Mrs. Vargrave said, heartily. Then Cecile got herself away, and wrote as follows:—

"MY DEAR MRS. HEPBURN,—Our stay at Penzance depends on that most variable of all things—a woman's will. Aunt may issue marching orders to-morrow. I am very sorry to hear of your health and Glene not agreeing, and of your being such a distance from Castlenau, &c. I do not know anything of Mr. Scorrier's mother. Have you any well-founded suspicion as to her selling mackerel here, which I can endeavour to verify for you ? Perhaps you may be intending to have that frail fish direct from a Penzance purveyor ! "

Then she wound up by asking Mrs. Hepburn to believe her to be " Mrs. Hepburn's very faithful

" CECILE VARGRAVE."

About the same hour that Amelia was employed in writing to Miss Vargrave, Mr. Scorrier was busy with a letter to his mother. The last sentence in his long weekly letter to her is the only one which need be copied here :—

" I have been working harder at business during the last few days than I ever worked before even at pleasure, in order that I may the sooner feel free to run down and see you. Don't be astonished if I drop in upon you in a day or two.

" Your affectionate son,

" ARTHUR."

He must have made up his mind when to go,
even while thus writing with apparent uncertainty; for the next morning, when Amelia met
her husband at breakfast, after his usual summer morning stroll about the grounds of Glene
and the village of Danebury, almost the first
words he said to her were—

"Where do you think Arthur Scorrier is off
to this evening?"

"I don't know; but I do know where I wish
to be off to," she said, quickly. "I am sighing
for the sea. I do wish you would take me to
Penzance."

Mr. Hepburn's face fell.

"Any other part of the coast—I dislike
Penzance. That's where Scorrier is going, and
I thought him foolish, for really it is a singu-
larly unattractive place."

"Oh! Mr. Scorrier is going there, is he?"
Amelia said, carelessly. "How sudden he is
in resolution, and movement too! Hasn't he a
mother, or an aunt, or something living there?"
and then she opened "The Times," and feigned
to dismiss the subject from her mind. Still,
as she had made up her mind to over-rule her

husband's "senseless antipathy" to the only
place on the coast to which she had the most
remote intention of suffering herself to be
taken, she read the dead-season articles with
but a wavering eye and a wandering mind.
"It shall not all go smoothly as a marriage-
bell just yet," she thought, bitterly; "and they
shall not be free to laugh together over my
weakness and want of change of air." Then
she finished her breakfast very quietly, feeling
very well satisfied with herself for having written that letter to Cissy over-night,—she had
placed it in the letter-bag on her way in to
breakfast, and being an accomplished fact it
was a powerful weapon.

"I have already written to Cissy Vargrave,
telling her I shall be happy to join them there
—as was agreed before I knew you had some
aversion to Penzance," she said. "The climate
would do me good; but never mind; I shall
get strong at Glene, without doubt, in time."

"The climate at Torquay would suit you
better," he said, anxiously, "or the south of
France. Amelia, I will have no trifling with
your health: it is much to me that you should

be well and look well; your friends will think
you are unhappy."

"Oh! my friends," she said, impatiently;
"if I don't feel well and look well, I really
shall not make what my friends may think
about it my greatest trouble." Then she went
away abruptly, leaving him to ruminate on
what would probably be her greatest trouble
did she neither feel nor look well.

Later in the day, while she was loitering
about after luncheon, wondering wearily what
she could do with herself to pass away the
long hours until dinner—not only what she
could do with herself this day, but the next,
and the next, and so on through an apparently interminable vista of time—Mr. Scorrier
came up to see her before he left the
place. She could not help infusing more
than the former hauteur and stiffness into
her manner when she saw him approaching
her. For she had not expected to see him
this day—she had not expected to see any one
in fact; and being deficient in that genuine
love of the beautiful which induces a woman
to dress herself to the best of her power on

all occasions, she was conscious now of looking dowdy, almost slovenly. Moreover, she was puzzled at the inconsistency on his part which had made him pronounce her to be in good health the night before, and brought him to see her in his medical capacity the morning after. Consequently she met him stiffly and haughtily, bowing to him politely, but not offering him her hand.

" I have come, at Mr. Hepburn's request, to see you before I leave Danebury for a week or two," he explained.

" I am quite as well as I can ever hope to be while I am dull and bored," she said, gloomily. " I understand now the bitterness of the complaints you made against the stagnation of your village life the first time I saw you."

He laughed : " I was a discontented dog then ; now I fancy that, under some conditions, I should find my village life pleasant enough, if I had a settled interest there."

" You mean, if you had a wife," she said, quickly.

" Well, I think I rather meant if I had

landed property in the place; but I dare say a
wife, as you say, would do much towards recon-
ciling me to being only a tenant-at-will, and
that will another's."

"Take my advice and my experience," she
said, gravely; "don't follow the example of
your friend Mr. Hepburn, and take a London
girl for your wife. There are times when, in
spite of my having everything to make me
happy, I find the difference striking indeed—it
strikes me down, and I never had the craving
for excitement that was raging in all my young-
lady friends and acquaintances."

"Perhaps it is because you lead such an
utterly unemployed life," he suggested; and
Amelia did not thank him for the prosaic sug-
gestion.

CHAPTER VIII.

UNSETTLED.

To very few people is given the great grace of being able to stay where they are on a fine day and do nothing. If they stay where they are, they do something active or tiresome in cele-bration of the weather. Or if they do nothing, they go to some distance to do it. I have only known one Englishman who thoroughly appre-ciated sun-heat and repose, and he always found life a lovely thing when he could lie for hours on his own grass-plot and watch green lizards.

One morning the day broke in Penzance with almost exceptional splendour. The waters of Mount's Bay at once went into that brilliant royal livery of theirs which they invariably wear in the presence of the sun,—that livery of opal, and turquoise blue, and deep, deep green, which no British waters save those that beat the Cornish coasts know.

It was very hot—hot with a lazy intensity of heat that made some people long to lie down and let the day go on without thinking, and others long to be off on exploring expeditions. The Queen's Hotel was very full, consequently great excitement reigned as to whose claims would be recognized as just by the letters-out of vehicles of all descriptions. The Land's End, the Logan Rock, the natural granite faces, these were the chief bournes to which the hearts of weary tourists turned. The tesselated pavement of the big hall of the hotel was covered with hampers of all sizes, packed by experienced natives who know how very hungry and thirsty admiration of the beauties of nature is apt to make the wandering stranger. Every minute two-wheeled dog-carts, or wagonettes, drawn by one or two of the famous Cornish greys, pulled up at the door, and divers sorts of bipeds, in search of the picturesque, stepped into them and were lost to view.

None of the usual types were wanting. There

were the inevitable bride and bridegroom ; he, on
the strength of the novelty of their relationship,
hiring a much more expensive carriage than his
reason told him he could afford ; she, on the
same grounds, refraining from protesting, in the
mildest degree, against what she felt would be
the cause of sore pinching in the housekeeping
when they got home and were not ashamed to
pull each other up for extravagance. There was
the old parson in silk gaiters and broad-brimmed
hat, who was probably a don in his own land,
an archdeacon or a rural dean at least, but
who here, in the rush and hurry of tourist-life,
was simply regarded as a much be-daughtered
old gentleman, who might be deprived of his
locomotive powers without compunction, if only
the drivers proved venial. There were the un-
mistakeably hard-run London people, too tired
and pulled by the race of the last few months,
to show in their face or manners how genuine
their enjoyment of this comparative rest and
tranquillity was. There were the brace of Oxford
men spending their "long" together on a
walking-tour. There was the consumptive hope
of the family down here, in the Italy of England,

on a forlorn hope. There was the still young, jolly couple who, having married in their boy and girlhood, are now surrounded by a troop of big boys and girls, who call their parents by their Christian names, and are all clamorous to go in different directions. There was the single lady, the unprotected female, in dust-coloured barege and a Leghorn hat, who may be the English Rosa Bonheur, or one of our most popular authoresses, judging from the sketching apparatus and note-book she carries about her, to say nothing of the further evidence of the eternal absorption in the beauties of nature in which she indulges before people, and her unvarying austerity to all those whom the vicissitudes of hotel-life put in her path on the stairs. Lastly, there were the Vargraves, in the various stages of exhaustion and prostration from the heat, early morning as it was, still, after the manner of people out for rest and a holiday, battling fiercely and fatiguingly with each other as to how rest might best be obtained, and the holiday enjoyed.

"It does seem a shame not to go on the water on such a day," Isabelle said; "do get a boat with an awning, papa, and let us go."

"It seems a great mistake to be down here and not to see any of the mines," Mr. Vargrave said.

"Now I should propose our not tiring our-selves," Mrs. Vargrave put in, freshly; "if we could get a nice open carriage, and just drive to all the principal points along the coast, getting out and walking whenever we feel inclined, we should be turning this fine day to good account, I think; what do you say, Cissy?"

"I say—nothing," Cissy replied; "and that is just what I should like to do."

"Only we ought to make up our minds before every carriage in the place is secured by somebody else, if we don't follow your plan," Isabelle said, and then she went and leant her arms on the window, and watched some more departures.

Presently a well-appointed wagonette and pair of horses pulled up at the door. "An arrival," Isabelle said, as a gentleman sprang to the ground, and she caught sight of an elderly lady still sitting in the body of the

carriage; "it's your dove-coloured old lady of
The Crescent, Cissy," she was saying, when
she was interrupted by the waiter opening the
door, and announcing Mr. Scorrier.

He was a stranger to the old people, and
perhaps, had he called on them in this way in
London, they would have remembered that he
was a stranger, and caused him to remember it
also. But as it was, Mr. Vargrave (on whom
the responsibility of regulating all these
women's whims fell heavily) received him
pleasantly, as a man can receive a stranger
in a strange place, when he feels that he can
be quit of both as soon as he pleases.

"I scarcely expected to have the good fortune
to find you at home on such a day as this. I
came last night from Danebury; and having
heard that you were here, I thought perhaps
you would (if you had nothing better to do) go
and spend a short time at St. Michael's Mount
—it's well worth seeing."

"I have been seeing nothing else since I
have been here," Cecile said. But she did not
say it as if to see it closer, in his company,
would be wearisome to her.

"It would really be delightful to make a pic-nic there to-day," Mrs. Vargrave said, getting up and looking out at the grand Mount, as if it had never struck her before. And then it was proposed, and carried without a dissenting voice, that they should accept the unceremonious invitation and the impromptu pleasure, and that Mrs. Scorrier should be induced to come in and wait until such time as they could be ready.

She came in beaming, ready to like them all, and to strive to make them like her. With the clear-sightedness of a great affection she had seen, from the manner of her son, during the very little conversation she had held with him on this subject, that if his heart was not already given to, it was more than well-inclined towards this girl, whose graceful stateliness, and lovely face, had so favourably impressed her the other evening. The mother was more than ever anxious that her son should succeed in his suit, when the young lady came forward to meet her this morning; came forward with a flushing brow, for the thought that his mother might be hers some day would obtrude itself.

It would obtrude itself, though Cissy was not at all given to over-estimating the value or the meaning of masculine attentions. She was not one of those misguided ones who imagine that every man who suffers himself to be kind is striving to be tender; or that if a man sought her society, and took delight therein for four or five hours, he must be contemplating the best way of securing the same to himself through life. Still, though she was not one of this numerous and unfortunate class, she was a very woman in her power of penetrating into motives so transparent as Mr. Arthur Scorrier's. And she had thought of him a great deal since that day of Amelia's wedding, when he had scarcely stirred from her side all day. This— the having thought so much about him—and the feeling that now, on the first opportunity, he had brought his mother to see her, caused the flush to rise on her face. And the flush rising on her face caused the hope that he might win her, to rise more highly in his heart. Altogether they were both in an auspicious mood, and were not likely to disregard their privileges and opportunities during the

long sunny hours they were going to spend together at St. Michael's Mount.

She was prettier than ever. Prettier, far
prettier now, with the glow that was the off-
spring of the sea-air and the sun, and the
inner excitement upon her face, and in the ex-
quisite simplicity of her morning dress, than
she had been as he had seen her last—in the
elaborate bridesmaid's toilette, which had been
designed by Amelia. But if she contrasted
favourably with herself as he had seen her last,
how far more favourably did she contrast with
Mrs. Hepburn, as she had appeared before him
the day before, slovenly and out of spirits!
The brilliant, blue Swiss cambric, the daintily
delicate collar and cuffs, the carelessly arranged, but fastidiously kept, silky dark hair, and
last, but very far from least, the winning face
that would kindle at his approach, completed
his subjugation. He determined to win her
for his wife, not only if he could, but as soon
as he could. His heart swelled warmly as he
thought of the beauty and the grace of the
home he had made for himself in Danebury,
and of how she would add to and deepen every

charm it now possessed, when she became its queen.

The drive to Marazion, the village just opposite to that "Castle in the Sea," St. Michael's Mount, was a very pleasant one to them all, although the springs of the carriage were not too good, and they were strangers yet. But they started with the praiseworthy intention with which everyone should start for an outing on a summer day—they were determined to make the best of things, in order that they might give the lie to the old prejudice which deems it lack of wisdom to engage in any exploit which compulsorily binds strangers together, without full occupation for any length of time. "Cissy, his mother is evidently full of beneficent intentions towards you," Isabelle said, as soon as they were out of ear-shot of the room in which they had left Mrs. Scorrier, on their way to put on their hats.

"Perhaps she thinks my uncle's will be a nice, safe house for her son to spend his idle time in, when he is up in town," Cissy said, struggling hard to speak as she did not feel.

"You'd murder any one at this moment who

seriously accused a Scorrier of mercenary motives," Isabelle said, quietly; "you know you would, and I know it too. Well, dear, your fate has come,—that is, if you can make up your mind to bear Amelia's foot on your neck."

" She will never have an opportunity of putting it there," Cissy said, "even if I, or he, or his mother, or fate—for you're mixing us up all together—do the best or the worst you imagine."

" Never have on opportunity ! If you go and put yourself near the park-walls of Glene in an inferior position, my dear Cissy, you know her too well not to feel she will make the opportunity—and so do I."

" I don't want to discuss improbabilities ; and I don't want to keep any one waiting, so I'll go on," Cissy said, in answer to this. Then she went down, and in a few minutes more the Vargrave contribution to this pic-nic, in the shape of a couple of hampers—one of wine and one of provisions — and the Vargraves and Scorriers themselves, were packed away securely, if not comfortably, in the wagonette, and on their way to Marazion.

"And now we must hear all about the Hepburns," Mrs. Vargrave said, genially, when they were clear of the town. "Cissy had a most delightful letter from Amelia—that's Mrs. Hepburn—yesterday."

"Mr. Hepburn is Arthur's greatest friend," Mrs. Scorrier said, confidingly; "but do you know, singular as it may seem, we have never met!"

"Never met! dear me!" Mrs. Vargrave, who was not at all staggered by the fact, said, in a tone that implied the deepest interest. "Well, I have never seen him myself, but I have heard that, though he is much Amelia's senior (she was a girl with our girls, you know), though he is much her senior, he is a man whom any girl may esteem, even love."

"Whom have you heard that from, Aunt?" Cissy said, saucily; and then Mrs. Vargrave remembered that she had not heard it at all, that she had no stronger grounds for her assertion indeed, than the fact that she had once or twice expressed a hope that such might be the case. But she did not word this remembrance; she only shook her head with that air of playful deprecation which old ladies are apt to assume when they have nothing to say in answer to a direct question. Then she was saved further embarrassment by Arthur Scorrier saying,

"Whoever Mrs. Vargrave has heard it from, she has only heard the truth; he is a man whom any woman—any good, sensible woman—might find it easy to esteem and love."

"I do believe, if Arthur were his son, he could not care more for Mr. Hepburn than he does," Mrs. Scorrier said, looking round on them all with her eyes swimming in tears. "I always feel that there must be something quite superior about him, and it makes me regret so much that we have never chanced to meet."

"There is a prospect of your doing so now, Mrs. Scorrier," Cecile said. "You will be sure to see them if your son stays here any time, for Mrs. Hepburn tells me they are coming to Penzance—for her health, she says," Cissy added, turning quickly towards Mr. Scorrier, who sat at her right hand.

He grew scarlet as he answered: "I believe

they have given up the idea of coming to Penzance though ; he does not like the place—at least, he does not like to come to it."

And then poor old Mrs. Scorrier gave the reins to confidence and a desire for sympathy, and would tell them that Mr. Hepburn's dislike or disinclination to come to Penzance arose from a reason that did honour to his heart. "He was my husband's dearest friend and companion, and he saw my husband drowned in those very waters," she said, tearfully, pointing towards the bay. "It told on us so differently : I came to the spot that had seen the last of him, and have lived here ever since, and Mr. Hepburn got away, and can never bear to look upon it. Men and women are so different, are they not ?" Then there was a pause for a few moments; for when a tragical story has been told, no matter in what words, it is hard to go back to the commonplace at once. Mrs. Scorrier herself was the one to relieve them from this difficulty into which she had plunged them. She led the way back to a brighter path easily enough, by saying:

"So you see, though we have never been

personal friends, Mr. Hepburn and I, it is only natural that I should wish to see both him and his young wife. Such a trying difference in their ages," Mrs. Scorrier said, shaking her head in doleful sympathy with the tryingness of it. "Such a test, you know, for them both, as I say." Then the old ladies went on to call Mrs. Hepburn "a poor young thing," though in their hearts they did not pity her in the least; while the young ladies questioned Arthur Scorrier about the Glene *ménage*.

"Glene is a glorious place, isn't it?" Isabelle asked. "Amelia has managed to give us a vague idea of its grandeur—being about second only to Windsor Castle—in her letter of yesterday to my cousin."

"It is a glorious place; but I don't believe she cares about it," he said.

"There you are very much mistaken—she does care about it very much," Cissy said.

"When other people are by to be impressed by a show of such caring; but she told me the day before I came here that I was to be particularly careful, and avoid taking a London-bred wife to live in my country home." As

Arthur Scorrier said this, his eyes and Cissy's met, and each understood that the other distrusted Amelia Hepburn as far as they were concerned.

"There was a plan about our going to stay at Glene," Isabelle said, a little discontentedly; " but Amelia has taken it into her head that Glene is unhealthy because her 'medical adviser' says she needs change of air. I suppose her ' medical adviser' recommends what he thinks she would like."

" I am that distrusted individual," he said, laughing. " Glene is one of the healthiest places in the world; still, for all that, I don't think its air suits Mrs. Hepburn."

" Glene is a very ancient family possession, is it not ? " Mrs. Vargrave asked.

" Yes, very," Mrs. Scorrier answered, promptly. " I used to hear Mr. Scorrier speaking about it; he was as fond of Glene as if it had been his own, instead of his friend's; it has been in the family ever since the Conqueror, I believe, though it's not entailed, which makes the fact a prouder thing, I always think; it has gone on from father to son, from father to son, as regularly as if it had been bound to go so."

As Mrs. Scorrier brought her commendatory mention of Glene, and the way it had been handed down from generation to generation, to a close, the carriage pulled up at the door of the inn in Marazion, where they learnt that fate favoured them in the matter of the tide being out sufficiently to admit of their walking over to St. Michael's Mount.

It is not all easy pleasure getting to St. Michael's Mount. If you watch the hour of the tide being out, you can walk to it over a rocky road, and shatter your unaccustomed feet to pieces against boulders. There are a few retainers' and fishermen's houses at the foot of the Mount, and a few boats lying about, to take the unwary who suffer themselves to be caught by the tide back to Marazion. When these dwellings are passed, the tough ascent commences, and it is sufficiently of the nature of a precipice to make one wish that the lord of the castle, who is doubtless a model of courtesy, would have a lift, such as is used in lofty hotels, for the benefit of invaders upon the grand seclusion of this castle by the sea.

Native helps, born to the fatiguing manner of this place, brought the hampers over, and led the way up the slippery path among rocks which lead to the first platform, from which twenty cannon bristled at them. Then a long uneven line of roughly-hewn steps showed them the way to a little iron-girded black oak door, which is the chief entrance. Much of the romance of the place is brushed off when that narrow entrance-door is passed; for though there is a good deal that is antique and interesting about both the architecture and furniture inside, there is nothing that corresponds to the rough, grand majesty of the exterior of it.

They followed the ordinary routine, went into the guard-room and gazed at the helmets, and old stirrups, and bridles and cuirasses, and tried to feel interest, not to say pleasure, in the result of such gazing. And then they went on to the Chevy Chase room, and uttered ejaculations over the three-hundred-year-old arm-chair, and the five-hundred-year-old bed-

stead, and looked at the niche in the wall
where the skeleton was found some years since
—another illustration of the kissing crust and
warden pie and naughty nun story. When
they had done all this—"wasting precious time
in the doing it," Arthur Scorrier thought; for
while the tour of inspection lasted he could
get no private word with Cecile Vargrave—
when they had done all this, they went out on
to the grassy slopes, where broad patches of
borage in full bloom gave pleasant promise of
claret-cup to come.

Presently the pair on whom the chief interest
of this story is designed to centre found themselves apart from the others, down low among
the rocks, where the waves were beating. How
they got themselves apart it is not easy to say;
though, judging from the celerity with which
they did it, they found it an easy thing to do.
As they neared the margin of the water, he
pointed out a hollowed space in a rock that
"might almost serve for an arm-chair," he said,
and there she placed herself, whilst he stood
over her, watching her graceful good looks with
appreciative eyes, until he longed to claim them

for his own. There was no use in dallying
with opportunity. From a thousand signs,
brief as had been his acquaintance with her, he
had taught himself to believe that he was a
little more than another to this girl. They
were together now; but how, unless something
could be assured, some ground made securely
his own at once, how might it be after this day
was past? She would go back to her kaleide-
scope life in London, and in the enforced
contemplation of its ever-changing pattern and
hues, would naturally soon cease to think of
the country surgeon who had stood by her side,
and watched the waves beating on St. Michael's
Mount. " She shall not forget me—whatever
comes, I will put it out of her power to forget
me," he thought, stung by the fear of such a
possibility. And all the while he was thinking
these things, Cecile was talking to him about
the view, and the heat, and the coming
luncheon.

"Won't you be glad when we are called up
to have something to eat, Mr. Scorrier? I shall;
because I have said all my sayings about the
freshness of the air, and the beauty of the

scene ; and it has been hard work, because you have not given me a helping responsive word."

"No, I shall not be glad when we are called up to have something to eat," he said, sitting down by her side, looking at her so intently that she fell to playing with the brim of her hat to cover her embarrassment. He was re-membering Mrs. Hepburn's caution to him against seeking to win a London girl for his wife, and wondering if he could win her, how this brilliant creature would live a prosy village life. Suddenly, he had no doubt or fear about what might follow, if only he could win her. Suddenly, he resolved to try at once.

" Were you displeased with me for coming to-day, and for bringing my mother ?" he asked.

" How should I have been displeased, or anything but well pleased ?" she answered. " In the barren wilderness, would not one wel-come a foe, much more a friend? Mrs. Scorrier saved us from a family dissension this day by bringing us here ; they all wanted to go dif-ferent ways, in order to properly enjoy this mar-vellous imitation of a southern summer day."

"And what did you want to do?" he said.

"To stay where I was—until you came."

The words were very few and simple, but they contained a world of meaning to the man who heard them.

"And when I came, you were content to quit those plans—to break up and alter them for me?"

"Yes, for you and your mother."

He did not quite relish the conjunction, still he could not complain of it. But it threw him back a few minutes, and every minute was precious, since, if once interrupted, this *tête-à-tête* might not be secured again.

"Could you have done what your friend Mrs. Hepburn has done?" he commenced, abruptly—"have given up the town-life of change and variety and excitement, for the almost unvarying solitude of the country?"

"No, I couldn't."

"You could not? it would be too great a sacrifice."

"Far too great a sacrifice," the girl said, shaking her head solemnly.

"Then I will try to get something in London," he exclaimed; but she only glanced at him quickly, and went on:

"I could not have done what she has done for several reasons: in the first place, love and sympathy are more essential to me than they are to her, and I could never expect either from a man who might be my father; or if I got them from him, I couldn't give them in return, and that would be unpleasant."

"But could you do it for the sake of one who could give you love and sympathy in return— could you do as she has done in that case?"

"In that case I should not be called upon to make any sacrifice."

"You would not feel it to be a sacrifice—a sacrifice beyond the power of making; you could do it—you will do it?"

"I could do it," she said; and then he possessed himself of her hand, and she would not return his pressure while she was saying, "but I would not do it if it involved an equal sacrifice from the one for whom I make mine."

"Make it for me," he said.

She was ready, ay ready to make it for him. He felt that by the way in which her pliant form swayed towards him; he read it in the glorious, softened glow that spread over her face. She could make a sacrifice gloriously, for it was in her to make the one for whom she made it feel that he was the one who obliged by accepting it.

" It would be none if made for you," she said, in a low tone.

" Then you will make it—you will be my wife ? " and now he grew into an agony of anxiety for her answer to be given him before that summons came to luncheon, which might cut into the midst and upset the nearly made arrangement.

" I can't say yes, dearly as I would like to say it; there is so much to be said to you before I ought to bind you by assenting myself. You have your way to make in the world—you must not be clogged."

He began to pray and protest, to claim and use his right to caress which her acknowledged love had given him. But she kept him off.

" No, no !—not till you have heard what I have to tell you, and convinced me that it need be no obstacle to our marriage; " her brow blazed as she said this, and she looked so strong in her beautiful pride for him, that his love rose higher than ever.

"When may I be told—when may I convince —— "

"They are calling us—come!" she said. "We will come here again by-and-bye." Then they went up to the platform to dinner.

CHAPTER IX.

SETTLED.

It had been very tedious to these two young people to walk through the castle in the wake and under the observation of others, therefore it may be supposed by some people that it was to the full as tedious to sit down in a space between some overhanging rocks and have luncheon in the society of others. There would be great reason in such a supposition; for has it not been told that they had just been saying and thinking many things that were emotion-engendering? However, appetite is a great king, to whom nice emotions give place very often, and in spite of what had just gone before, they did not find the luncheon-time tedious by any means.

Indeed, on the whole, Cecile regarded it

as rather a relieving interruption to a most
thrilling occasion. For all her light nature
and light training, and still lighter habit of
life, the girl had a quick, keen sense of honour,
and it did not seem to her that she would be
obeying its dictates in receiving and recipro·
cating the vows of a man who was not perfectly cognizant of who she was, and how she
was situated. That he should know these
things in time, before she finally accepted
or rejected him, she was quite determined. But
it was a hard matter to tell off glibly, without
more prelude than had yet been played, the
dubious story which was to be told about herself. " If he can take me with the shade over
me that is over me, and will never reflect on
my mother, I will go to him," she thought ;
" but not else, and not while he is ignorant or
merely tolerant." And then she remembered
that there was yet another impediment to this
marriage scheme which he had laid before her
this day—remembered more than this, that she
had no money, and no hopes of ever having
any money, and that he was a "poor struggling
man " (*vide* Amelia Hepburn's letters concern-

ing him and other things at Glene) who could
not afford such an encumbering luxury as a
penniless wife.

"He shall not be mortified; I will tell him
all this by-and-by, and then in reason he will
be obliged to confess that I am wise in saying
it can never be." So she thought, eating her
chicken and lobster salad, and sipping her
claret, enjoying these delicacies with the keen
appetite that was born of the sea-breeze, and
that refused to be impaired by all these sorrowful doubts concerning her future.

For she was very sorrowful in the thought
of having to give him up. That which he had
thought, or affected to think, a sacrifice on her
part, did she agree to his proposition, would
have been no sacrifice to her. She could take
up her abode " anywhere, anywhere, out of the
world " or in it, under certain conditions, with
the most perfect and complete reliance on her
own power of making herself happy and comfortable. A life in a country village, or in a
London centre or suburb, or in Ireland, or in
Egypt, would be all one to her, provided those
conditions were fulfilled. Love, peace, and

rest would bring happiness and contentment even to her restless heart and soul. "If I were only everything to a man, he should find that he was everything to me," she thought. Yet she was not ready to say he should be everything to her, until he had shown himself to be indeed regardless of some things which she felt bound to tell him.

Luncheon was over at last, and then Mr. Scorrier began to look impatient, and as if he thought it was quite time for them (for her and himself) to get back to their old station under the cliffs by the sea. But the opportunity which she had so confidently declared she would make, delayed itself. In the first place, the helps who had brought their hampers over were not conversant with the heady nature of sparkling wines when taken under a burning sun; consequently, the effects of the large ends of bottles which they had with some forethought reserved for themselves, became apparent in sundry inefficient and futile efforts to pack up the *debris.* "If we don't clear this up for ourselves, it will never be done for us," Cecile said. "Come, Isabelle, let us make a beginning." Then Isabelle, who was tired with the delights of the day, and who had no pleasant love-making to look forward to after she had cleared up, consented slowly, and proceeded to help her cousin and Mr. Scorrier, whose annoyance at the delay caused him to be very much of an obstacle and stumbling-block in Cissy's path.

At length the last fork was found, the last hamper was secured, and then Cissy stood up, pushing her hat back off her temples, and declared herself to be very warm and exhausted. "I shall just go down and dip my hands in the sea and cool my forehead," she said.

" Sea-water put on under a broiling sun like this will tan you terribly," Mrs. Vargrave remonstrated. But Cissy was bent upon cooling her brow in the way she had mentioned, and when she went away in the direction of the rocks, Arthur Scorrier followed her. Mr. Vargrave and Isabelle were contented with cooling their brows from the summit of the battlement platform, and old Mrs. Scorrier and Mrs. Vargrave remained alone.

It would show great ignorance of human

nature generally, and old-lady nature particularly, if it was asserted and believed that these two elderly gentlewomen did not immediately proceed to confidences. Every circumstance attending them, every condition of hour, time, and place, were in favour of their doing so. And they did it.

"It always makes me sad to watch the ·waves for long," Mrs. Vargrave commenced. Now it never had made the excellent lady sad for one moment before in her life, but just now she felt languid and sleepy, and so she believed herself to be speaking the truth, and nothing but the truth, when she declared herself to be feeling sad.

"So it does me," Mrs. Scorrier responded, quickly; "but then my great sorrow ·comes from the sea—from this very sea that is rolling before us, in Mount's Bay too."

"I had not heard of it before to-day," Mrs. Vargrave said, gravely.

"No, I dare say not, though it seems to me strange that any one should be at Penzance for an hour, without hearing the story that is told to me at the corner of every street where I can

catch a glimpse of the water." Then Mrs.
Scorrier told the story over again of her early
desolation through her husband's drowning—
told it with quiet pathos and very few tears,
"and I knew nothing of his family, and have
never heard of them since; I have been cut off
from the poor comfort even of their sympathy,"
she wound up with.

"But what comfort you must have in your
son," Mrs. Vargrave said, saying it rather because she could not think of anything else to
say, than from any strong conviction on the
point of Arthur being a comfort to his mother.

"I have, indeed," old Mrs. Scorrier said,
kindling to the theme; "my only comfort, and
only pride in life; but he will soon be more to
some one else than he is to me—or at least
some one else will soon be more to him than I
can be or ever have been; we mothers must
look forward to that."

"I only hope he will choose well," Mrs.
Vargrave said, finding herself utterly unable to
avoid thinking of her own niece, in connection
with the subject of Mr. Scorrier's choice.

"I hope he will—well in every way; he is

my only child and hope, you know, and all my pride is in him. I never had any for myself, Mrs. Vargrave, but when he was born I began to be proud for him, and if I was proud for him as a baby, think what I must be now."

" Yes, of course," Mrs. Vargrave said, with a promptitude that was worthy of much praise, seeing that she did not see in what way Mr. Scorrier was worthy of a greater measure of maternal pride being lavished upon him than any other mother's son.

" But though I'm so proud and happy, and blessed in my boy," Mrs. Scorrier went on, warming to her topic, "I always feel what a thing it would have been to have a daughter." This was a graceful concession on Mrs. Scorrier's part to Mrs. Vargrave's claims to a right to have judgment also on the subject, though she had nothing loftier than a girl to exercise it upon. "My son has been away from me for years ; I should have kept a daughter with me till she married, and then my life wouldn't have been so lonely."

" But they all do marry, sooner or later," Mrs. Vargrave said, philosophically; " and before they're married they are thinking about being so, and absorbed in their own hopes and fears. Our children only take after us in that respect—we ought to remember that; it is natural, they wish to go, and they will go."

"Are you likely to lose either of your girls soon?" Mrs. Scorrier asked, with pardonable curiosity.

"I don't know that I am yet; and life is uncertain, and neither Mr. Vargrave nor myself are as young as we were. We should be very glad to see them settled, or to know they were likely to settle, and our principal anxiety is about Cecile—naturally."

"That is your niece," Mrs. Scorrier said, feeling very hopeful. She felt sure that now she was going to hear "all about that sweet Miss Vargrave," and that the "all" would transcend her expectations.

"Yes," Mrs. Vargrave said, settling herself down as it were into a more confidential position. "Cecile is my niece, or at least my husband's niece, and we know no difference in our feelings between her and Isabelle. "At least," the truthful lady continued, "we know very little difference between them; but it exists, and in one way and another it must be shown in time, and felt by the dear girl herself. I have always hoped that something or other would happen in business, you know, to enable Mr. Vargrave to give her the same as he is going to give Isabelle; but nothing does seem to happen as one could wish it in that way," Mrs. Vargrave continued, with vague amiability.

"And she has no parents," Mrs. Scorrier said, compassionately. The discovery that Cecile had no money, and would have no money, was an obstacle, though not an insurmountable one, to this union in her eyes. Doubtless the young lady came of a stock that would counterbalance all deficiencies of that sort. Arthur wanted other things more than money with his wife.

"And she has no parents."

Mrs. Vargrave shook her head, in the negative.

"Poor thing! Has she been an orphan long?"

"Her father died seven or eight years ago,

her mother later, I believe, but we never knew
her." Mrs. Vargrave stammered a little as
she said this, and grew confused, under a sense
of being sorry that she should have let herself
stray into a path of speech that led to Cecile's
mother. From which Mrs. Scorrier, unworldly
as she was, soon deduced the fact that Cecile's
mother was to be avoided, even though she was
dead.

"I think it is getting chilly here now the
sun is clouded," she said, softly; "shall we
walk down to the rocks and see the tide coming
in?" She rose up as she asked this, settling
her shawl over her shoulders, and moving a
step or two in the direction in which Arthur
and Cecile had gone some time before. Mrs.
Vargrave did not find it chilly, and did not care
about seeing the tide come in. But the "dove-
coloured old lady," as Cissy had called her, had
a quiet will of her own that was hard to resist.
Accordingly, the two matrons went down the
boulders directly, as far as they felt that they
could go with safety and comfort. When they
reached this point, the young people (Cecile
and Arthur) were still far ahead of them—out

on what looked like a perilous pinnacle of rock, with the tide all round them, save where one craggy ledge left a pathway—a difficult but safe pathway back to the Mount. The roar, light but unceasing, of the waves prevented them hearing themselves called. Perhaps, too, they were a little absorbed in the subject they were discussing.

"What could have induced them to go out there?" Mrs. Scorrier said, in rather a vexed tone; "young people are so thoughtless." But she wronged them. They had not been thoughtless in their selection of the position in which they had placed themselves. They had wished to secure themselves from interruption from any one less light of foot and steady of nerve than themselves, and they had succeeded in their design.

When Cecile had packed up the last plate and lashed up the last hamper, assisted by Mr. Scorrier, she had felt very full of confidence as to the ease and power with which she would revert to and settle the subjects he had opened before luncheon. But on her way down the rocky pathway to the water's side again, this confidence had failed her, and she began to wish,—first, that her task was over; secondly, that there had been no need for her to set herself such a one.

It may be remembered that almost the last words spoken between the young people before they had been called to luncheon, had been an entreaty from him that she would make the sacrifice—that she would be his wife; and a declaration from her that she could not say yes to this entreaty, " dearly as she would like to do it," until she had told him something that she felt she ought to tell him, and had been convinced by him that this something was in truth no obstacle to their union. Perhaps she was only too ready to be thus convinced. Perhaps she was going to be obstinate—obstinate with that most annoying of all obstinacy, which strengthens itself with the belief that it is for the good of another. He could not tell what she meant to do with him, and with herself, as he walked by her side back to the spot where she had promised to settle the question.

Nor could she tell what she meant to do with him, though she was not at all undecided as to

what she would like to do. As far as she could
judge, a marriage with him, while it would
satisfy her heart, would not involve a single
sacrifice of taste, or feeling, or custom. There
was nothing in the life she was leading now
which she would be false enough to feign to
regret, if she did after all leave it for him. It
was a gay and glittering life—more of the
kaleidoscope order, indeed, than Amelia's had
been while she was Miss Foster. Still, gay and
glittering as it was, it was eminently unsatisfactory, fitful, and feverish to Cecile Vargrave.
Things which she looked upon as attributes and
non-essentials were regarded and esteemed as
chief elements, and vital necessities almost, by
the people with whom she lived. Moreover,
she was always in the position of not having
her life in her own hands, and of being compelled to be extensively obliged to those who
regulated it as she did not like. Besides all
this, there was the ever-present sense of inse-
curity—a sword was always hanging by a hair
above her head—a thunder-bolt was liable to
fall upon her at any moment. The old weakly-
constituted story that always seemed to be

dying out, and that yet would not die, would rise up vitalized by other people's sense of honour and duty, when the occasion arose. This she had always been given to understand, and she had accepted the inevitable, and been grateful to those who spared her such a resuscitation while they felt they could. Still it had always been a spectre in her path, and she could not bring herself to feel that she could ever regret leaving a society in which it mocked her from every corner.

Now the occasion had come, and she was going to be brave enough to attempt the resuscitation herself. She would not leave it to her uncle and aunt; they would try to revive it with too great a tenderness—a tenderness that would put the man for whose benefit it was done at all, in the painful position of having his generosity appealed to. So she went down prepared to handle it boldly, roughly even, if she saw need to do so; and the determination to do this made her path over the rugged rocks a terrible one.

"Not here," she said, when they reached the spot where they had been sitting before luncheon; "we're too close and hemmed in here, and I should fancy some one behind me, and on either side, and should be hampered in my speech, and I don't want to be hampered; let us go out further."

So they went out further, stepping over little chasms, and wading through little shallow pools, until they reached the place where they were eventually seen by Mrs. Vargrave and Mrs. Scorrier.

"And now, what are you going to say to me?" he said, as they stood clearly outlined at last.

"I thought I had a great deal to say," she answered; "but it all amounts to this, and can be said quickly—I should like to be your wife, but I can't be."

"You shall be, whoever comes between us," he said, hotly, taking her hand. Her words conjured up the vision of an accepted rival in his mind, and Mr. Arthur Scorrier was quite determined to crush and disregard the claims, however well established, of any such superfluous being.

"Hush! listen to me," she said, a little imperiously; "it's nothing of that sort that you mean. I am as free as air in that way, but I am fettered still; you have asked me to be your wife on the strength of seeing me as I seem to be, not as I am. I live with my uncle and aunt, and have their name, and am treated in all respects as their daughter is treated; but I'm a sham;" and now her violet eyes were lifted up half boldly, half beseechingly towards him, "I'm not a Vargrave—my mother was never married."

"That was no fault of yours," he said, tenderly, clasping her hand more closely than before, though a quake respecting his own mother's feelings on the subject passed over him as he spoke; "that must not stand between us. Why, if you had erred instead of your mother, I should love you, and want you just the same."

"You would be weak in that case—you are only wrong now; indeed, indeed, you are wrong. How could it be well for you to take a wife with a stain on her, and no money to compensate in the lightest degree for it : that's the plain hard truth—that, if I didn't feel you deserved the most honest treatment from me, I could never bring myself to word. I'm a penniless, illegitimate girl—that's the long and the short of it; and doesn't it sound horrible?"

Again she looked up at him, and this time her eyes were full of tears.

"As you say, that is the long and the short of it; and now let there be an end of it—will you be my wife?"

"You ask me that again, because you feel bound in honour to yourself not to desert me for my misfortunes, without giving me another opportunity to mend them, which I could not be mean enough to take."

"You could not do anything mean, and you are not going to try to do anything to make me miserable: marry me, Cissy."

"Ah! men don't believe that a woman can understand the point of honour; why I might, and surely should, be detrimental to you," she said, quickly.

"How do you know—I mean what makes you cling to such a misguided notion?" he said.

"Reason, and a certain hardly acquired know-

ledge. Now look here; my life hasn't all been
spent in Bayswater, under the wings of my dear,
careful, kind uncle and aunt. I led a nomad
existence for a good long time after I was sufficiently grown up to attract attention. My mother
used to be very, very restless; she could not
bury her dead and feign to be satisfied and
happy while living under a cloud; so we used to
wander about, and we were not good managers,
and did not always bear ourselves at Boulogne
as we did at Baden; and some way, as such
things do leak out, it leaked out that we were
not of the order of the Philistines; that we
were, in fact, Bohemians; and people fought
shy of us, or were insolently intimate, and the
end of it is, I have had to suffer that which it
is well your wife should never have suffered.
What a fearfully long speech I have made," she
said, in a different tone.

"And a purposeless one, Cissy, darling, if you
think that it is going to alter my choice and
intention," he said, firmly.

"No, not a purposeless one; for I am
strengthening myself in my resolution by re-
calling these incidents; they are so unlike

whatever happens to me in my quiet life now, that it makes me feel as I think of it all, that I can't be the same person who went through them."

" Well, rest and be thankful that the nomad existence is over," he said ; " forget it, or if you like, look back upon it as a page of romance, the reading of which will occasionally relieve the monotony of Danebury."

" I'm sometimes uncertain whether I am thankful that it is over ; I'm a vagabond at heart, and that life was more to my taste than the one I lead now. That is another argument against my accepting your offer—I might sigh for the old times and old habits ; I should never sigh for the thoroughly respectable visiting and weariness I have had in London."

" You are making difficulties," he said, half laughing. " I would take you to some of your old haunts—I love the Continent quite as much as you do—and you should look upon them from a new point of view."

" From which I should be expected to be ashamed of them; no, that wouldn't do. I should never feel anything but sympathetic about

foreign vagabondism, and it's hopeless to try
to make me think that I should do so; but you
would be justified in feeling disgusted, if people
that I couldn't and didn't wish to keep at bay
in those days were free and easy with me; it
wouldn't do.   Give it up."

"Never," he said, smiling; "if any one of
whom I disapprove is too free and easy with
you, I shall know how to protect you."

"But I mightn't wish to be protected.
Though I might not think the free-easiness
proper, I mightn't object to it; besides, Amelia
Hepburn, though she does not know all I have
told you, suspects a good deal, and she would
never spare me in an English country neighbourhood.   I should move about weighted with
the knowledge that I was suspected of having
been guilty of a miscellany of iniquity."

"Now I shouldn't have thought that you
were a girl to regard puerilities of that sort," he
said, with a sort of good-humoured authorita-
tiveness that she felt it was not at all bad to be
subjected to.   "What does it matter what impression Mrs. Hepburn has given of you or
gives of you?—she could never counteract the

impression one sight of yourself makes; besides, how can you bring yourself to put up these people, of whom you have never even so much as heard, as barriers between us?"

"And I shouldn't have thought you were a man to argue on false premisses in that way," she said, half laughing. "I don't know the people about you now, I allow, but if I went among them I should know them; and as for Amelia, she would soon (if we were thrown much together) have the power of making me very miserable; she would thinly veil the feeling that you were very much to be pitied for something, and I should understand her and feel a culprit."

"Since you have no better reasons to adduce for thinking it advisable to make me unhappy, I shall not allow you to put them up as obstacles. You shall tell me you will marry me, and brave all these trifling annoyances for my sake: all that you have told me has only made me love you the more—it is settled."

He said this just as his mother and Mrs. Vargrave came down to look for them—or rather just as the old ladies made their voices

heard by the young people. "They are wanting us; we are keeping them," Cecile said,
turning and beginning to retrace her steps hurriedly.

"Give me your hand," he said, taking hers
without waiting for her to give it to him; "the
rocks are slippery—you will fall. Now say it
is settled before we rejoin them; I cannot go
back in the state of uncertainty you compelled
me to be in all luncheon time; say it is settled
as I wish."

"I feel I am being fearfully imprudent and
selfish," Cissy said, softly.

"That is not definite enough for me. I
want to hear you say that, between us, it is
settled that you are to be my wife."

"As far as I am concerned then—yes!"

"And you only are concerned," he said,
earnestly. "Whom does a man marry—the
girl herself, or her family, or friends, or foes?
You only are concerned. You have made me
so happy by this promise, Cecile."

"What if I should break it?" she muttered.

"You would not be so cruel—I was going to

say you will not be so base," he said, reproachfully.

"Not of my own will, or for my own
pleasure; I love you, and it will go harder
with me than with you, if others make me feel
that I may do you an injury by wishing to
stay with you and love you all my life. One
favour,—quickly, Arthur,—don't speak of it to
any one till we have talked together again."

"There is no good in delaying," he urged.

"But I insist—I beg rather, you will not
speak of it till after seeing me to-morrow, at any
rate."

"I suppose it's as well to promise that, since
it's settled," he said.

CHAPTER X.

"ONLY YOURSELF TO BLAME."

THOUGH they had to the best of their ability settled the great question which must of necessity be a vexed one to every unsettled man and woman, it is a fact that they did not experience any great sense of elation on their way back to rejoin their friends. Arthur Scorrier did make an opportunity, in getting Cecile over a chasm, to press her hand most reassuringly. But the assurance conveyed in that pressure was not quite strong enough to overpower all her considerations as to what her own people and his mother would think of her, for having suffered herself to be led away into what looked very much like a solitary flirtation.

"What a goose they will think me!" was her inward reflection, as she stepped up on the

ledge where Mrs. Vargrave and Mrs. Scorrier
stood.

"You have got yourself most terribly sun-
burnt—quite red, Cissy," Mrs. Vargrave said,
complainingly, turning round and beginning to
toil up the pathway without delay. Mrs. Vargrave saw that the solitary time on the rocks
which the young people had passed had, for
some reason or other, not been quite pleasing
to the mother of the one who might be looked
on as the executive power. "And no one's
mother shall think I want to throw either of
my girls at her son's head," she thought.
Accordingly, she spoke reprovingly to Cecile
regarding the sun-burn, which was nothing
more than a blush, and altogether deported
herself as one who had a right to feel aggrieved.

There was a slight, a very slight, but still a
perceptible change, too, in Mrs. Scorrier's
manner, Cissy found. "The dove-coloured old
lady" had lost a shade of the soft, soothing
tone which had seemed to be all over her
before. She spoke kindly to Cissy still, but it
was with a stiffer kindness than seemed well to

the girl who had been treating the old lady's
son so very openly and honourably.

"I shall really feel quite glad to get back
home, and have a quiet cup of tea with Arthur,"
Mrs. Scorrier said; and when she had said
that, somehow they all understood that it had
been in her mind at one time during the day
to propose their all spending the evening
together.

"I hate tea," Arthur said, "and no amount
of quietness makes a cup of it endurable to me;
does it to you?" he added, appealingly, to
Cissy.

"No; but then I don't like comfort and
quiet, and tea and respectability," Cissy said,
defiantly; "as I told you just now, I'm a
vagabond at heart."

"I think, if Mrs. Vargrave likes, we had
better be getting back now, Arthur," Mrs.
Scorrier said; "by the time we reach Penzance
we shall have had a nice long day."

"A very long—I mean a very nice day,"
Mrs. Vargrave said, promptly; "yes, I should
like to go now." And then they met Mr.
Vargrave and Isabelle, and walked away to-

gether to the landing-place, for the tide was in now, and they would be obliged to go home by boat. As they went, Cissy possessed herself of her uncle's arm, and hung upon it for refuge, as it were; and somehow even he felt that all had not gone quite well with some members of the party.

" Don't let yourself veer away from me on any pretence whatever," Arthur said, warningly, to Cissy, while he was seeming to hand her into the boat; "you are mine now, and I won't allow any vacillation."

"I am in a great state of bewilderment—a confusion of ideas respecting wrong, right, and myself; and I haven't even a 'little dog at home' on whose decision as to my identity I can rely. I can only trust to myself, Arthur."

By the time she had said this, the old ladies, and the hampers, and the now utterly incompetent helps from Marazion were adjusted in the boat. In another minute they were off, pulling against a ground-swell and a wind that was dead against them; feeling that wind and tide were literally against them—against their

separating and getting rid of one another, as
all fondly desired.

Arthur Scorrier loved his mother dearly,
and considered her on all occasions very much.
But now he felt very angry with her as they
drove back to Penzance. It would have been
so easy for her to propose some scheme to offer
them some little civility which would have kept
them together all the evening, and enabled him
to gain further speech with Cissy. From being
angry with his mother, he grew angry with Mr.
and Mrs. Vargrave. They, at least, might have
invited him to stay an hour or two at their
hotel. That would have been a very usual and
proper *finale* to such a day. As it was, it was
evident that the untoward constraint which had
crept into his mother's manner had affected the
Vargraves perniciously.

However, as it transpired, it was only Mrs.
Vargrave who was affected by that slight change
in Mrs. Scorrier. Mr. Vargrave was absolutely
unconscious of it, after the manner of men.
But he was tired by his day of refreshing quiet
and pleasure; tired by the meal that was
neither quite a luncheon nor quite a dinner;

and uncomfortably conscious that, in addition
to its having tired him to-day, it would have
a prejudicial effect on his constitution the next
day. But he no sooner came in sight of the
hotel that was his home for the present, and
smelt the invigorating odours of divers dinners
that were in a state of preparation about that
hour, than his joy in life and general geniality
returned, and he asked Arthur Scorrier to come
back when he had seen his mother home, and
have some dinner with them.

When the wagonette stopped, several idlers,
belonging to the visitors in the hotel, lounged
nearer to look at the party. Amongst these
was a face Arthur Scorrier recognized.

" Why, there is one of the Glene servants—
Mr. Hepburn's own man ! " he exclaimed ; and
then he jumped out and asked, " Is your mistress here ? "

" Master and mistress too, sir," the man
replied. " Master does not feel very well, and
has gone straight off to bed ; my mistress is
going to dine presently, and while she is at
dinner she wanted you to be sent for to see
master."

" Give my compliments, and tell them I shall be back in half an hour," Arthur said, quickly.

" Amelia here ! " Mrs. Vargrave exclaimed.

" How nice ! " Isabelle said, hopefully.

" How very funny ! " Cissy added.

" Then I shall make the acquaintance of Mr. Hepburn at last, and under most auspicious circumstances," Mrs. Scorrier said, beamingly, forgetting her constraint and the cause of it in an instant.   Then the Vargraves said good-bye to her, and got themselves into the hotel, and Mrs. Scorrier and her son drove on to The Crescent alone.

" You won't stay with them late to-night, will you ? " she began, coaxingly.

" I don't know what you call late, mother."

" Well, not too late to see me before you go to bed.   I have something to say to you."

" Put it off till the morning, there's a dear mother," he said ; " I shall be weary enough when I get back—not fit to listen to you."

" But I always think no time like the present, and you could take the night to consider whether my advice was worth following or not

—and tell me what you make your mind up to in the morning," she persisted.

"If it's advice, I will certainly not hear it to-night," he said, laughing. Then they were home, and he excused himself from hearing more by running away, first to dress himself, and then back to dinner at the hotel, leaving Mrs. Scorrier in a tumult of feeling, that was partly fluttering fear that her son might go beyond the point at which it would be honourable to pause,—go beyond that point this night, and tell her in the morning that he stood pledged to marry Miss Vargrave, and partly fluttering pleasure that at length there was a chance of seeing the man who had been her husband's companion and her son's friend.

While this tumult of feeling was still fresh upon her, Arthur was hearing what had brought the Hepburns to Penzance. He had got himself ushered straight to Mr. Hepburn's room, where he found that gentleman lying on his couch, though he was apparently in no less robust health than when Arthur had seen him last at Glene.

"I heard you had gone out for a day's fool-

ing at some pic-nic place," he said, in answer
to Arthur's question about his arrival and
seclusion, "and as I didn't want to be let in
for meeting a lot of people whom I don't know,
and don't care about, I gave out that I should
go to bed, and came here to be quiet; Mrs.
Hepburn is with the Vargraves, I believe."

"You altered your plans rather suddenly,
didn't you, sir?" Arthur Scorrier asked;
"when I left Glene the day before yesterday,
you had no intention of coming here."

Mr. Hepburn seemed to be a little put out of
temper by the reminder.

"If it hadn't been for your professional
humbug," he said, "I shouldn't have been
here now; but Mrs. Hepburn insisted on your
having recommended change of air, and set
her heart on coming to Penzance; there was
nothing left for me to do, for I couldn't let her
come alone."

"No; that would naturally have nullified
the pleasure she might otherwise expect,"
Arthur Scorrier said, with an air of unlimited
faith in the connubial felicity of his old
friend.

Mr. Hepburn reddened a little, and assented slowly to the proposition.

"Not but what she was most kindly anxious that I should not sacrifice my own desire to stay at Glene, or to go somewhere else; but the fact is, she has set her mind on Penzance —it's her old friends, the Vargraves, being here that made her wish to come—and I would never thwart a woman if I could avoid it; so, though she would even have put up with the disagreeables of a journey, and stay here alone, I preferred coming with her."

"I dine with the Vargraves, and it's their dinner-hour," Mr. Scorrier said, looking at his watch; "you won't stay here all the evening?"

"I don't want to see a number of strangers," Mr. Hepburn said, testily. "Who have the Vargraves got with them?"

"They are alone."

"I thought I heard they had gone to a pic-nic with some old ladies."

"Only one old lady, my mother; and she has gone home."

"I hope Mrs. Scorrier is quite well," Mr.

Hepburn said, politely; "don't be late, my boy; I shall go out and try the sea-breeze by-and-by, and then we'll meet again."

Arthur left him with that, and went off quickly to the Vargraves' sitting-room, where he found dinner ready, and Mrs. Hepburn comfortably seated. She held her hand out to him as he came into the room, but did not rise, or in any way disturb the *pose* which she had practised beforehand, and heard from Olive looked a positively regal one. All traces of slovenliness had vanished. She was splendidly dressed, rather too splendidly, perhaps, for a quiet evening at a sea-side hotel. The two Misses Vargrave, in plain high white muslins, looked under-dressed by her side.

"If we had known that we should have the pleasure of your company, we would have made different toilettes," Mrs. Vargrave said, feeling compelled to apologize for her own *foulade* to the wearer of such a mauve satin and Maltese lace fichu. The lady of Glene smiled a smile of one who could afford in her plenitude of luxury to be tolerant to all those who were lacking.

"I am a matron now, and I think it would be bad taste of me to wear girlish dresses in preference to such matronly garments as these," she said, touching her satin and lace: "I always study suitability."

"I'm afraid you'll distrust the suitability of that dress by-and-by, when we go down to the railings by the sea, and the spray comes dashing over you, Amelia," Cissy said, laughing. Then Amelia looked at Mr. Scorrier, and smiled and lifted her brows, as if she would give him to understand that she saw through this envious cavilling at her costume, but was too indifferent to resent it.

Mrs. Hepburn was not at all averse to the prospect of going down by moonlight, and walking along the esplanade, or leaning on the iron railings in company with Arthur Scorrier. She had several things to say to him, and she had quite made up her mind to say them this night. Not a doubt assailed her mind as to her power of carrying the important point of securing his sole companionship. They would all go out together; and once outside the door, she would plead that delicacy of health which he had given as an excuse for ordering her change of air—she would plead this, and ask him for his arm. There would be nothing but what was proper, safe, and reasonable in such a request; for was he not her medical adviser?

But the judgment of the just is often very much in error. When at length the move for the moonlight promenade was made, Arthur Scorrier attached himself to Cissy Vargrave's side, in that unmistakeable way which gives parents and guardians the preliminary shock. Accordingly, Mrs. Hepburn was condemned to take her exercise, supported by Mr. Vargrave alone, and Mr. Vargrave had never liked her much when he had known her a girl with his own girls; and he disliked her excessively now that she was a married woman, well inclined to exert her prerogative, and tax his powers of politeness to the utmost.

For awhile the four—Mr. Vargrave, with Mrs. Hepburn on his arm, Mrs. Vargrave and her daughter—kept near together, and the other pair sauntered on a few yards ahead of them in front. But after a turn or two, Mrs. Hepburn took to being tired, and to finding the sea-breeze very strong. "Are there no other walks in Penzance than this?" she asked, as plaintively as she could. "I do feel the need of air so greatly, and yet I can hardly bear this breeze; isn't there some walk with trees, that may remind me of my own Glene?"

Courtesy commanded that Mr. Vargrave should immediately think of all the places in Penzance wherein trees grew, and calculate whether they were within the walking powers of the lady. As he hesitated, she helped him. "I think I have heard of The Crescent, as a nice shady place. Mr. Scorrier's mother lives there. I have heard him speak of it."

So they walked off in the direction of The Crescent, mentioning where they were going to the others as they passed them.

"What on earth are they going there for?" Arthur Scorrier exclaimed, in undisguised annoyance. "I think we had better go after them, for if my mother happens to be out for her airing they will meet, and my mother will grow ecstatic over that anomaly."

"You don't like Mrs. Hepburn," Isabelle said.

"No, I can't say I do like her; she's a treacherous woman—a woman who won't commit a fine, well-developed treachery, because she never has a well-developed end in view, but who will take you unawares about a host of minor matters; she's engaged in doing some one now—though who it is I can't say."

Mrs. Scorrier was walking along on the pavement in front of number nine, and presently, in the natural order of things, she met the Vargraves and Mrs. Hepburn, and also (this to her annoyance) her son and Cissy. The sight of the two latter slightly acidulated her bearing, as it were, and rendered her less ecstatic than her son had feared she would be at this first sight of Mrs. Hepburn.

"The name has been a household word with me for so many years that I am delighted at length to see one who bears it," she said, holding out her hand to Mrs. Hepburn. And Amelia felt constrained not only to take the hand, but to infuse a certain amount of civility into her manner of taking it. For though the old lady was unconventional and unworldly, there was a certain sweet earnestness about her

that quelled Mrs. Hepburn's desire to be kind
in the grandly patronizing way she had
sketched out, as the manner to be adopted to
Mr. Scorrier's mother until it could be seen
under whose banner the latter meant to enlist.

" And how is Mr. Hepburn ? " Mrs. Scorrier
asked, with that air of deep anxiety which is
often displayed by old ladies when inquiring
after the health of the most indifferent person.
But in this case it was not an indifferent person for whom the inquiry was made. Mr.
Hepburn had been a hero of romance—a
guardian angel—a great unknown to Mrs.
Scorrier during all the years of her widowhood
—for it was a real heart-widowhood, that of
hers, though the little ring of gold had been
wanting to make good her claim to the name
of wife. It seemed to bring her very near to
him—very thrillingly near to him—this meeting with his wife. Still, when the first gla-
mour had passed away, his wife looked so
young and altogether so different from what
she had expected of the wife of the great unknown, whom she had venerated vaguely for so
many years, that he receded from her again;

and she began to feel that he was too shadowy for her ever to derive real tangible comfort from him.

But though Mrs. Hepburn would have regarded Mrs. Scorrier very lowly as an end, she thought well of her as a means. Thereupon she interposed between the old lady and the dying hope—the hope that at last the guardian angel would be seen by her in the flesh.

"We shall be here for several days, I think," Mrs. Hepburn said, as sweetly as it was in her to say anything. "Come and see us; and then you will see how Mr. Hepburn is for yourself."

Then, after a few words, more or less idle, they went their several ways; and again the feeling of acidulation set in in Mrs. Scorrier's breast. Again her son Arthur walked away in the unmistakeable manner that has been already commented on, by the side of the girl who would have been a delightful daughter-in-law if only it had all been clear about her mother.

"We have both been very wrong in devoting ourselves to each other as we have done," Cissy said to Mr. Scorrier, as they walked home. "But it's well to do wrong sometimes, and one can always pull up and be prudent ; which you must be pleased to be after to-night, for ' a chiel's among us taking notes.' "

"After to-night there will be no need to be prudent," he said.

" That is as I may think," she said, quickly; " but there are others to be consulted besides ourselves."

" Not in such a matter as this."

" Yes ; even in such a matter as this—of a marriage between us," she said, coldly. " It's not all conscientiousness this on my part—at least, some people would give it a harder name. But the fact is, I could not bear to be looked coldly upon by any one."

" And who would dare to look coldly upon you now ?—and will you crush me by hinting that any one would do so the more for your being my wife ? "

" Your mother looked coldly on me to-day, from the moment we met after luncheon," Cissy said, quietly. " I can put cause and effect together. My dear good aunt opened her heart about me under the influence of the sun and the lunch to Mrs. Scorrier; the result of this unburdening of her spirit was, that Mrs. Scorrier learnt a goodly portion of the tale I told you, told gently and kindly, as Aunt Vargrave would tell it; but I saw the effect it had; and I didn't like it."

" And you could, for one moment, contemplate giving me up, because of that nonsense?" he said, almost angrily.

" I am not sure, on the one hand, that I do contemplate giving you up; and I'm not sure, on the other, that I do regard it as nonsense. But just this I am sure of—that I won't go a step further till I know it won't hurt you in any way with any one; and now you mustn't attempt to answer me, or the others will hear you." With that she stepped on quickly and joined the others, and they all went into the hotel together.

A messenger met them, wishing them all to adjourn to Mr. Hepburn's room. He had engaged the first saloon on the first floor, and was sitting in it now in sombre splendour. He had refrained from going out, much as he longed for fresh air, on account of one or two of his prejudices, as his wife called them. But though he had made up his mind to stay within, he had not at all contemplated spending a solitary evening. Some thoughts had evidently been galling him deeply, for he looked worn, almost haggard, when they went in, and Arthur Scorrier noticed that he replied almost coldly to Amelia's inquiries as to his welfare— inquiries which she made with an undue display of conjugal anxiety.

"Well! how should I feel well?" he said, querulously; "the soup they brought me, after great delay, was cold, and the wine is boiling; did you ever taste such fire-water?" he continued, pushing a bottle of sherry, which stood on a pier-table at his side, nearer to Mr. Vargrave.

"It's the best philosophy to take things as they are when one is travelling," Amelia said, deprecatingly.

"You took a very different tone when we were at the Lakes," he said, quickly; "there nothing was good, and you never failed to mention the fact."

"I didn't know then how perfect Glene was

in its power of compensating for all little ills
and vexations," she said, good-temperedly.

But Mr. Hepburn would not accept the good-
tempered explanation. For the first time since
their marriage he was suffering himself to show
displeasure towards his wife before people. And
this first sign of such forgetfulness of others
shows a forgetfulness of her which no wary
wife would do well to disregard. But Amelia
Hepburn was not a wary wife, though she was
a very wary woman. The wifely wariness is
born of love and a desire to please her husband,
as much because so to please him is a pleasure
to her, as because it is a duty. So now Amelia
was unobservant of the sign, and proceeded to
put him in an untoward rage by what looked
very like obtuseness. In answer to the politely
pretty little platitude which she brought herself
to utter respecting Glene, because of the anxiety
she felt to get well away from the discussion of
Mr. Hepburn's present sufferings and inconve-
niences at Penzance—in answer to this polite
platitude he only said, " Judging from your
manner while you were there, my dear, no one
would have supposed Glene had been fortunate

enough to gain your approbation," and it must be confessed that his tone as he said this was not a pleasant one. Amelia glanced towards Arthur Scorrier as if she would have claimed his sympathy. But he would not return her glance, as in the first place he did not feel any sympathy for her; and in the second place, had he done so, he would have been the last man in the world to show it under these circumstances. Accordingly, Amelia was thrown back upon her own devices to make the best of it, and her own devices led her into another unpropitious path.

"Mrs. Scorrier is not a bit like you," she said, addressing Arthur Scorrier; "I should never have supposed you were her son."

Mr. Hepburn looked up quickly.

"Have you made Mrs. Scorrier's acquaintance already, my dear?" he said.

"Yes; and she is coming to make yours tomorrow," Amelia replied; and then, though the light in the room was not great, Arthur saw that Mr. Hepburn's face blanched.

"He is thinking of my father," the young man thought, compassionately, and he was

right. Mr. Hepburn was thinking very uncomfortably of Arthur's father. The word "uncomfortably" may sound hard and unsympathetic,
but it is the only word that can at all express
the varied sentiments that thronged Mr. Hepburn's mind, as he thought of the one whom
Mrs. Scorrier mourned daily as she looked out
on the rolling waters of Mount's Bay that had
been so evil to her.

"Yes, and she is coming to make yours to-
morrow," Amelia had said in reply to that
question of his as to whether she had " already
made the acquaintance of Mrs. Scorrier."
After this reply a sufficiently awkward calm be-
fell them ; each, evidently, had too much relied
on one another as far as the gallantry required
to make a fresh constitutional start was concerned. Happily, after a short time, Mr. Vargrave recalled St. Michael's Mount to his mind,
and proceeded to discourse fluently on the grand
structure. Then, by the time the grandeur of
the structure was exhausted, he called another
fact to mind, namely, that they (the majority
of them at least) had been indulging in the
dubious delights of a pic-nic, and that, there-

fore, they might be permitted to feel fatigued. When this point had been ceded to them amicably, they all rose to go, and Amelia stood up to take leave of them with a queer sense of prostration upon her. She had intended to say so much to Mr. Scorrier this night, and she had said nothing. Might it not be that this trip to Penzance, which had already been productive of domestic dissension, should be altogether a failure? She would not pause now to consider what right she could have to think it a "failure," if the "sea-breezes strengthened her," and "she saw a good deal" of the Vargraves—for it was by the power of these pleas that she was here at all. She would not pause to consider what right she had to consider it a failure; she only felt "that, after all, if things went on in this way," she should have reason so to think.

As she shook hands with Mr. Scorrier she said, "I had a return of my faintness to-day; I should like to see you to-morrow, before twelve."

"At any hour you please," he said, gravely, and then they parted.

As soon as his guests were gone, Mr. Hepburn, who seemed strangely weary and feeble for so strong, and active, and hale a man, betook himself to rest. But while he was waiting for his man, he roused himself sufficiently to say a few words to his wife, words that made her burn with anger, and declare to herself that she was unjustly treated.

"I feel very much annoyed at your having sought out Mrs. Scorrier in this way, Amelia; it implies an eagerness to get more intimate with her son, of which I cannot approve."

"You have only yourself to blame about him," she said. And her words cut deeper than she thought.

CHAPTER XI.

MOTHER AND SON.

THERE was an air of patient expectation, of quiet waiting, about both his mother and the room in which she was sitting, when Mr. Scorrier reached home, that was infinitely irritating to him. He saw at a glance that it was in her mind to exert her maternal prerogative at last, and to call him to account for that which he had done, or that which he might be about to do. That he would bear this patiently was his firm resolve. He felt that it was due to her that he should be so patient—due to her, simply as a slight return for the long unceasing indulgence of, and belief in him, which had made his home-life a happy one to look back upon. "She never found fault with me, or hinted that I might do better or other than I did," he reflected, and the reflection softened him, and made him deal gently with the phase of feeling which dictated the course she was now pursuing.

Old as she was, there was something that was very attractive and pretty still in the eyes of men, in Mrs. Scorrier's colouring and expression. She had the soft, bird-like hazel eyes, and the thin silky hair of the same colour, that always appear to be the outward sign of gentleness and tranquillity in woman. Her complexion was still fair, too ; her skin soft and unlined. Time had touched her very gently, perhaps out of compassion for her, and antagonism towards fate, which had been so rough to her.

This night she looked a little older than she had ever looked before ; a little older and a little sadder, and it went to his heart to see her look so, though he could not regard himself as the cause of the slight change blamingly. He determined to notice and attribute it to the pic-nic.

"My dear mother," he said, making a small bustle with the neat little plated bedroom candlesticks that were put out ready for use, "not gone to bed yet after this tiring day? I must talk shop to you, and advise instant retirement, or I shall be having you very poorly tomorrow."

"Not before I have said a few words to you, Arthur," she said, pleadingly; "I must, my dear—they lie so heavy on my heart, while they are unspoken—let me say them."

"Why should you ask for my permission? You will surely say what you like," he said, gently.

"Not what I like, but what I ought to say. Arthur, I only think of you, and of how your happiness and honour may best be secured." And then, as she thought of the old, bitterly-repented of error which had wrecked her own honour, and tarnished her child's, she bent her head, and her tears fell fast.

"Mother, what causes this?" He went over and caressed her, putting his hand on her shoulder, and kissing her still unwrinkled brow. "You are exaggerating some little mistake until it forms a misfortune before you; I can have done nothing to give you such grief."

" I have looked forward to the time my son would marry as the time that should bring me the greatest joy I can ever hope to know," she replied. " I have prayed for him to choose wisely, and to give me a daughter I could welcome as such."

"I have chosen wisely." His tone was very loving, but very firm.

"Not if you have chosen Miss Vargrave," she said, impetuously. And now it seemed to him that the sweet old tone that had sung lullabies to him in his cradle, and told him fairy tales in his childhood, had lost much of its sweetness. " Not if you have chosen Miss Vargrave," she repeated, for he was dumb.

" I have chosen her, and I have chosen well," he said, decidedly, recovering himself, removing his hand from her shoulder, and gradually, so it seemed to her, withdrawing himself from her.

" You cannot know what I do about her, about her parentage," she said, blushing freely, as she broached the topic before her own son.

"I know everything."

"And you will marry a wife with no name, or a stain on it; and I can never, never——" she stopped, sobbing over the broken dream— the dream of going back to the old eastern county homestead with her son, and some born gentlewoman as her son's wife.

"I do not see that I am specially called upon to visit the sins of the fathers upon the children," he said, impatiently, at last; and she shuddered at his speech, though she had forced it from him by her treatment of the subject. At last she raised her head.

"Have you made your choice known?"

"Yes, I have. Come, mother, this must not breed misunderstanding and ill-feeling between us. If you cannot welcome Cissy as a daughter, the woman does not live whom you will welcome as such; whether you will ever be privileged to welcome her, is an open question. I could combat the prejudices and opinions of all the world for her; but whether I shall be strong enough to combat hers successfully or not, I do not know yet."

"Hasn't she accepted you?" Mrs. Scorrier

asked, with quick, motherly pride, looking up and drying her tears.

No—that is to say, she has accepted me conditionally; but an adverse word or look from any one whose right in me she allowed, would deter her from taking me; I know it would. I feel that my. happiness and worldly welfare hangs on a hair," he continued, excitedly.

"You would not further that welfare by a marriage with her," Mrs. Scorrier said, persuasively; "there is no idea of her having any fortune from her uncle. Mrs. Vargrave told me so plainly; but that would be nothing, nothing. But I have hoped all your life that your wife, when you had one, might add to your claims, not cause you to be looked down upon and perhaps slighted; for the world is so hard, Arthur, so hard;" and then memory assailed her again, and she bent her head away to conceal the tears that were falling fast from her soft, sad, hazel eyes.

"The world may be as hard as it likes—it can't affect my love."

"That is the romantic view of it, but it

does affect the love of the nearest and dearest —it makes a woman hide from her own for years, because she will not see them look reprovingly ; and it may make her live a lie, and be hard to her children."

" Mother, you are speaking of what happens in the case of a woman who has erred herself, not of one who is blameless; we are not responsible for the faults and follies of one's parents.

" But we suffer for their sins," she said.

" I will leave it for others to be judges and accusers, and self-constituted dispensers of divine wrath," he replied ; " what there is sad and painful about her mother will never affect Cissy's relations with the nearest and dearest. Those she lives with could not love her better if she had been born in the purple; and my devotion, if I can win her, shall compensate her for what she may lose through the narrow-mindedness of others."

" You will not hear me," Mrs. Scorrier said, weeping freely now, and wringing Arthur terribly by her tears ; " but you will listen to Mr. Hepburn—he, at least, knows the world, and you will believe him if he tells you that this will injure you."

"Yes, I will hear what he says, but I can't promise that what he says will make the slightest difference in my intentions."

"And do you think that you are justified in taking a wife who will necessarily add much to your expenses, and not bring you a penny towards them? You can't live upon love in these days, Arthur, and with your habits, and, perhaps, with a family about you very soon, you may get into debt, and then all comfort will be over."

"If I get into debt, I'll work and get out of it; but there is no reason with my present income, and an increasing practice, why I should get into debt."

"If you do, you cannot look to her relations to help you. I feel sure of that—Mrs. Vargrave said as much to me. They are fond of their niece, but they will do nothing to hurt their own daughter's prospects, for the sake of a niece who has no legal claim to the relationship; and where you are to look for help I'm sure I don't know. I would pinch and screw, but all the pinching and screwing in the world would not enable me to give you more than would be a drop in the ocean of your house-keeping."

"You are going very much out of your way to face evil for me, mother," he said, laughing.

"I take the common-place and practical view of the case, Arthur," she said, seriously. "So much money was sunk in buying the practice, and furnishing the house, and I know your income cannot be very large. I suppose I must not ask what it is?"

"You may ask, and I will tell you, with all the pleasure in life; I clear eight hundred a year."

"And with some wives you might live most comfortably on it," the old lady said, meditatively.

"I shall be quite contented with one—Cissy Vargrave."

"What can she know about housekeeping?" Mrs. Scorrier inquired; "men with only eight hundred a year, in these days, want a wife who can do more than sit gracefully at the head of the table, and dress beautifully. What can she know of housekeeping, or of how far money will go—brought up abroad, where there is no management at all, I should say? The end is certain. You will have no home-comforts, and you will be in debt into the bargain, and all my hopes for you will be blighted."

"Well, we will not say any more on the matter to-night, mother," Arthur said, jumping up. "We must never quarrel, whatever comes," he continued, putting his arm round her again, and leaning his head down on her shoulder, "my own dear mother, we must never quarrel."

"No, never; never—but oh! Arthur," and then she drifted off into tearfulness again, and so they parted for the night.

Mrs. Scorrier went to bed and pondered deeply, asking herself seriously what would be the right thing for her to do in this crisis, and striving earnestly to make herself give a truthful answer to the question. It has been told that by her blameless, obscure life, she had obliterated the memory of her early sin and sorrow from the minds of those who had only heard vague mention made of it, and nearly obliterated it from her own. But the memory of it came back freshly to her this night. She had stirred the fading embers of the fire of remembrance, and it blazed up and almost consumed her in the night. "Perhaps I ought to tell him all, and throw myself for mercy on his judgment," she thought. Then even her feminine illogical mind warned her this would hardly be the right course to pursue, while her heart shrank from the thought of being lowered in the eyes of her son. She dared not even tell him her story as if it were the story of another; she felt she dared not. By some trick, some tone, some trembling, or some allusion, she would surely betray herself if she attempted it. So at length she went to sleep, resolving to seek Mr. Hepburn to-morrow, and ask his aid.

Her son lay awake too, but from a very different cause. The only point in his mother's argument against his marriage which had struck him as really strong, was that wherein she pointed out to him the exceeding probability of his getting into debt. Simultaneously with his vivid recollection of this point, he had an equally vivid recollection of what Cissy had told him relative to the nomad life her mother and herself had led abroad. Deeply in love as he was, reason told him that she had not been brought up in the best school for the education of a middle-class British matron.

CHAPTER XII.

A STRUGGLE FOR FREEDOM.

WHEN the Vargraves had got themselves back to their own quarters, and Mr. Scorrier had taken his leave of them for the night, they still lingered about, unwilling, as it seemed, to quit the cool balconied room, through whose open windows the sea-breeze played so temptingly. Moreover, in addition to the tempting nature of the sea-breeze, there was another detaining cause that was felt, though not expressed as yet. They were a very united family, and a feeling was in their midst now that something was to be said by one or more of them to-night to the others. Presently this feeling was worded by Mr. Vargrave.

" We seem to be sitting here for some purpose which does not come off ; don't you think we had better go to bed, all of us ? "

"Oh! no, uncle, not yet," Cissy said, quickly, and then she went over to him, and sat herself on the arm of his chair, and whispered, "I want to tell you something."

He was a very considerate man; one who would never enforce the hearing of a confidential communication upon any one whose presence had not been solicited by the confiding communicant. So now he asked in a low tone,—

"To tell *me* something, or to tell your *aunt* and me something?"

"Aunt and you," and she turned round and held her hand out to Mrs. Vargrave, who sat near, "that is, if she will stay up and be bothered with my troubles."

"Then I think Isabelle had better go to bed," Isabelle's father said, and Isabelle rose up yawning, and saying,

"Yes, I can wait till by-and-by to be told what I guess already." Then she went out of the room, laying her hand lovingly on Cissy's shoulder as she passed, making the latter feel that they were all glad, because they thought that she had glad tidings to give them about herself.

" Now, what is it, Cissy ? " Mr. Vargrave said, looking at her with that mingled air of amusement and embarrassment which men are apt to assume, when a girl is about to read them another page from the old, old story.

" I suppose, properly speaking, I should have left it to Mr. Scorrier to tell you this. But I preferred doing it myself, in order that I might be quite sure that it was done in the way I wished. He has asked me to marry him, and I am not clear that I ought to do it."

" Do you wish to do it ? "

" Yes," she said, emphatically.

" Then why not ? "

" Why not ? Would you ask that question if he were your son ? "

Mr. Vargrave, not feeling quite sure of what he would have done under these unlooked for circumstances, held his peace.

" You see," Cissy said, waxing very earnest, and forsaking that stronghold of calm in which she had taken refuge from herself during the term of her residence in her uncle's house, " I wish to say ' yes ' so very much, that I'm afraid of doing it until I have made sure that ' no, never,' ought not to be my answer ; I know there is a good deal against such a marriage for him. I know his friends will feel that there is much."

"He has only his mother," said Mr. Vargrave.

"Ah! uncle, don't speak in that way, and make me think you want me to go from you, whether I feel I am right in going or not. He has only his mother—I know that ; and I know that he is much to her, and she is much to him. If I marry him, I shall come between them. I can't help myself. She will think he ought to have done better, and I shall resent her thinking so; and that is not all."

"My dear Cissy, you are making mountains of molehills," Mrs. Vargrave said, reproachfully.

"And if I am, the molehill may be the greater obstacle of the two ; you can scale a mountain in time, whereas a molehill may trip you up, and kill you at once."

"Let us hear all your objections against this marriage, which, you say, you wish," Mr. Vargrave said, quietly ; " you have not stated all, you say ; go on."

"The other relates to means."

'He knows you have no fortune?" Mr. Vargrave said, quickly.

"Quite understands—realizes it fully—knows that, not only I have no fortune, but that I'm penniless, or, rather, farthingless."

"Then the question of means rests with him; if he thinks himself in a fit position to marry a woman without money, he, doubtless, is justified in doing so. I would never countenance an improvident marriage, but, if he is situated as I believe him to be, no objection can be raised on that score."

"But, uncle, consider. I can bring no grist to the mill; and let me be sparing as I will, I may be a log to keep him from rising, because I do not know how to spare in the right place; now, I will link my objections together, and ask you, as a man of the world, and a business man, and a man who knows the value of money, shall I be right in giving myself and my heritage of shame into his care and charge?"

"I did not know that you had suffered your mind to dwell so strongly on that misfortune, Cissy," Mr. Vargrave said, sadly.

"But I have, for years ; ever since I learnt

why my father and mother did not live together, like other girls' fathers and mothers; ever since I knew the meaning of her meek bearing whenever she met English people, and they were rude to her; how could I help my mind dwelling on it? how could I help feeling that the time would come when I should have to smart for it? It has come now."

" But, really," Mr. Vargrave said, fidgeting about in his chair, and wishing with all his heart that the time had not come on this special evening, when he was feeling very much worn out with the beauties of St. Michael's Mount; " but, really, if you married him, you would not be so prominently before the world as to challenge your position being questioned; if Mr. Scorrier is fully aware of all the disadvantages under which you believe yourself to be labouring, and, being aware of them, loves you well enough to disregard them and wants to marry you, I think——"

" Me Quixotic," Cissy interrupted.

" Not exactly that; but, perhaps, a little too keenly alive to the claims of *noblesse oblige*. If I say there is no objection to the man him-

self, and his means are such as to justify
him in taking a wife, and you like him well
enough to do it, there will be nothing, in my
opinion, against the marriage."

"Well," Cissy said, "that is coolly trans-
ferring the difficulty," and then she could not
help laughing as she told her uncle that he
appeared to have forgotten that it was of herself, and of her own position, that she had expressly stated herself to be dubious; not of Mr.
Scorrier at all."

"The time will come when both Scorrier and
you will thank me for telling you that, sensible
girl as you are, you are talking like a little
fool now," Mr. Vargrave said, good-temperedly,
rising up as he spoke, and so showing them
that he wished the conference ended. Then
they went their several ways; Mrs. Vargrave
looking in upon Cissy in her room a little later,
to kiss, bless, and advise her, and, presently,
to take it for granted that the affair would
arrange itself to the music of wedding-bells.

"And your summer holiday never need be
the slightest expense to you, my dear," Mrs.
Vargrave said, solemnly, as if the doubtfulness

of a summer holiday being feasible was the
one drawback to the match in Cissy's eyes.
" Our house will be your home whenever you
can come to it; and as for dress, dress costs
just nothing at all in the country; besides, you
shall go to him with such a *trousseau* that he
shall not have to pay for any of your clothes
for some years."

" You're so good, aunt; but I'm really not
quite sure that I'm going to him at all; but
if I do, I don't think my self-respect will be
wounded if he does supply my hob-nailed
boots and the few other trifles I may want
when I'm out of the world," Cecile said, in as
serious a tone as that in which her aunt had
spoken.

" And, after a time, his mother will be as
pleasant as possible to you; take my word for
it, she will," Mrs. Vargrave said, prophetically
and reassuringly.

" She will never have an opportunity of
being anything but pleasant to me," Cissy said,
drily.

" If you take my advice, dear, you will leave
off telling of what you used to do abroad.

Quiet English people think it strange when you tell them you had a pair of princes to tea with you, and that you went out and fetched some slices of ham for them to eat, yourself."

" I dare say they do think it strange," Cissy said, laughing; "they try to picture the Prince of Wales and the Duke of Cambridge dropping in, in a friendly way, to tea with people who live in lodgings along the Brompton Road, and their fancy refuses to treat the subject realistically. Well, aunt, I'll bury my dead—I mean, omit to mention my princes; but they were such little princes that I might be forgiven them."

Then Mrs. Vargrave—feeling that now, as Cissy had taken this tone, nothing tangible could be arrived at between them this night—retired to rest, and Cecile was free to think about what she had done, and what she had better do. The result of her reflections will appear, illustrated by her conduct, during the course of the next few days.

" You have only yourself to blame about him," Mrs. Hepburn had said, with reference to Arthur Scorrier, when her husband had re-

buked her about him, and Mr. Hepburn girded
against the remark in his heart, feeling that it
was only too true.

Nevertheless, though he thoroughly accepted
the truth of her saying, he was very angry
with her for having said it. The weeks had
not been many during which Amelia had been
his own. But, few as they had been, it is a
fact that he found her a very terrible possession already. She was very quiet, and very
self-contained, still, and subdued in voice and
manner. But, for all these things, she was
wanting in that gentleness which he began to
think now was the characteristic he most
prized in women. She was still, but she was
not soft—indeed, it may be averred, on the
contrary, that she was hard—hard as iron,
and not so malleable as iron, since no amount
of warmth would make her bend. He felt
that she had it in her to be very harsh and
bitter to him, if it ever seemed to her that he
had done her wrong in any way. Paris and
its pleasures must have got very much into
his head, he told himself now, before he thought
of taking that tall, unbending, cool young

woman to be the light and glory of his heart and hearth.

This question began to vex him sorely; was he not one who deserved to be punished, inasmuch as he had disregarded nature, and lightly considered their respective ages when he first proposed a marriage between them? "Crabbed age and youth cannot dwell together," he knew on good poetical authority. But then, again, his was not "crabbed age," or, at least, it would not be crabbed age, if it were given fair play, and not unjustly crossed, and lightly esteemed. His reason told him that he had been an old fool in taking this girl, in the hope that she would irradiate his declining years. His declining years would be dim indeed, he felt now, if they were not irradiated by some light on which more reliance could be placed than he could bring himself to place on his Amelia. She puzzled him—perplexed him sorely by that quick variation of manner which she had displayed towards Arthur Scorrier. Mr. Hepburn had watched her small attempts at first to play *grande dame*, and patronising lady-gracious to the young village surgeon—marked them with pain, and something which would have been contempt had not his wife called forth the feeling. Still, the change in her was unaccountable, and so perplexing and disagreeable. "Hunting up his mother, and throwing herself into the arms of an intimacy that doesn't promise anything that she can care for!" he said, impatiently; "the world will be less lenient in its judgment than I am."

Meanwhile, lenient as he believed himself to be in his judgments respecting her conduct, he was very cross in his bearing towards herself this night. He made life wearisome to her by the bitterness of the complaints he made about the climate and cookery, the accommodation and air of Penzance. "Besides," he added, "there is something infinitely distasteful to me in being dragged into these small sea-side acquaintances; it's all very well for grocers, and the like, to come down to these places and grow hilarious over the bad hotel-wines at their customers' expense, but it is not my style to have people in to refresh themselves in my drawing-room after their horrible pic-nics."

"You mean the Vargraves," she said; "I

am sorry that my friends should be so obnoxious to you."

"All vulgar people and vulgar customs are obnoxious to me," he replied.

"Vulgar! That word at least does not apply to the Vargraves."

"I acknowledge that," he said, waving his head and his hand with lofty condescension; still I have not been in the habit of people 'dropping in,' as they call it, and I don't like it."

"Yet at one time ——" she paused abruptly. She had been on the point of reminding him, that at one time Mr. Scorrier had been in the habit of "dropping in" in the free and easy style, which he now found objectionable, at Glene.

"At one time what?" he asked.

"Oh, nothing; I was thinking it was almost a pity that we had not a fairer understanding before we married," she said, suddenly.

"It was a pity, a great pity, if you feel the very slight obligations I would lay you under to be burdensome; we can never hope to lead happy, comfortable lives together, while you bitterly resent as injuries my most moderate requests."

"No, we cannot." She had turned half aside, and now stood with her shoulder towards him, and her head bent a little away. "We cannot, we cannot," she repeated, as it seemed mechanically, and then she faced round again, and said—

"But cannot we live apart? Assign any reason you like for the separation; say it's my health, or temper, or anything you like. Cannot we live apart? I will be contented with a very moderate allowance;" and then she began to speak fast and earnestly. "A very small certainty will suffice me—only make it certain, and me free."

"Never! You shall not make me ridiculous, and yourself conspicuous; you have done me a great wrong, a great wrong," he repeated, querulously. "But I will not cast you off, or leave you to yourself."

And then Amelia knew that, let what would come, she must abide the issue.

CHAPTER XIII.

A REQUEST AND A REFUSAL.

THERE had never been the faintest shade of romance over either the anticipation of the marriage, or the marriage itself, in Amelia's mind. Nevertheless, she had believed that there would be something very tangibly good and satisfactory about it. Broadly she had asserted—when her parents had remonstrated with her upon the improvident spirit displayed in that offer she made of utter renunciation of all Mr. Hepburn's worldly goods, provided he died and she married again—broadly she had asserted that she "did not care for love, but that she did care for luxury." Now she had luxury—luxury of the most blameless and respectable order. But it was cut too carefully after a pattern she did not like for her to be satisfied with it, and when she tried to escape, it was shown her ruthlessly that there was no escape for her.

One little sentence that her husband had uttered after she had made her ineffectual struggle for freedom, rang in her ears during all her waking hours that night. " We must make the best of each other, for I will not consent to be made ridiculous by your going away." This he had said, and this she felt quite sure he had meant. He would not let her go, even if she sacrificed all the coveted things for which she had married him. He would not let her go, and yet he would not love her the better for her remaining. But he would keep her with him, because it was his right so to do ; because her staying was more conducive to his dignity than her going would have been.

She was not an impulsive woman. Indeed, judged by the whole course of her life, any one would have been justified in pronouncing her to be an entirely reasonable woman. Her end and aim, such as it had been, had always been kept steadily in view by her. She had achieved it in her youth; achieved it without compromising one of the traditions which she had been brought up to esteem; achieved it at an age when most girls are hazy in their minds as to what they want to do with themselves— far more how to set about doing it. But now something else had come to the hard-natured woman, who had never wasted one foolish hour in receiving or paying attentions that were not likely to tend to a good matrimonial climax. Something else had come, and all the gloss was brushed off her early triumph.

" He will worry me out of my life," she thought, turning about in her restlessness; " and I have nothing to take off my attention from his worrying ways." Then she grieved over the absence of some of those small domestic cares and annoyances, which are frequently serious crumples in the rose-leaves of happily-married women. She remembered how her own mother had often found a servants' quarrel, and the difficulty of adjusting the same, a counter-irritant when some serious sorrow was impending. But at Glene she was too far away from her servants for her ever to regard them as other than mere serving machines. She did not tell herself so in so many words, but she felt strongly that for her, there was neither liberty, equality, nor fraternity.

As for the poor old gentleman whom she had married, he stood for less than nothing in these calculations which she was making respecting her own future comfort; or, rather, her future power of enduring his existence. Her most earnest hope respecting him was, that he would keep away as much as possible from the apartments which were more especially her own. One method of passing away the time occurred to her, and her heart beat a little more quickly with delight at the happy thought. She would get Mr. Scorrier to direct her taste in refurnishing and ornamenting a room—a boudoir—and she would make that room and its decorations the basis on which to build up an artistic and refined friendship with him. In that room, and amidst the surroundings which he himself had suggested, he should teach her to appreciate good books, and good art, and she would make herself essential to him as a real friend, in whom he could rely, in whom he could confide. To him, at least, she resolved to try to seem to be—

"A perfect woman, nobly planned,
To warn, to suffer, and command."

She felt that, given a sufficiently strong incentive, and she could become a very good woman —a patient, self-sacrificing, enduring woman. But even as she felt this, the thought smote her that the incentive could never be given now; would never be offered; might not be accepted by her, even if it was offered. She would never be permitted by fate and circumstances to warn and command one whom she could care for. All that there was for her to do was to suffer—to suffer and be as strong as it was in her to be.

They sat down to breakfast the following day, looking and feeling, to all appearances, very much as they had looked and felt every morning since their marriage. In reality, they were farther apart; for her entreaty to leave him at any cost to herself, had pushed him away from her; and, weak in his intense consciousness of the reason why she had married him, he could not summon up the requisite strength for the struggle, and try to get into her heart.

He could not summon up the strength to make the effort, and perhaps it would have been a mere waste of material had he essayed to do so. No skill, no strength, would ever make him more to that hard young woman, whom he had so liberally endowed with what she valued most in the world, than a tedious old man, whom it would take very little to make repulsive to her. He recognized this truth, or half recognized it, in all its hideous nakedness, as he sat at breakfast with her this morning; and though there had been no romance in their union, he felt cut and sore, old and contemptible. For another love had been given to him, without the giver staying to count the cost, when both he and she were young. He remembered this fact vividly now, and as he contrasted it with Amelia's coldness and hardness, his heart was smitten with a sad memory of that which he had cast away.

He was pleased for a few minutes to see that his wife had dressed herself with more care and taste for the breakfast-table than she usually bestowed upon her appearance when his eyes alone were to be gladdened by it. During her unmarried life she had been unwearied in presenting a fresh and fashionable front to the world. She had never permitted herself, in her hours of liability to others, to grow careless. But at Glene she had not had the incentive of strange or avowedly critical eyes upon her, to keep her up to the mark of being moderately careful in private, and her gorgeous toilettes—the toilettes that had been designed for the dinner-parties with which she had anticipated finding her career largely chequered—these were still doomed to silver paper and disuse. Consequently, she had lapsed into slovenliness, not being kept therefrom by any real innate love of the beautiful. But this day she had evidently made little efforts to look well, had studied sundry details of costume which hitherto she had neglected, and had obtained, in consequence of these efforts and studies, a fairer result than she had ever heretofore thought it worth while to put before him so early in the morning.

"Upon my word, you are very nicely dressed

this morning—very nicely dressed, indeed; that is quite my taste," Mr. Hepburn said, in a commendatory tone, glancing approvingly over Amelia's costume. Then he peered at it, and questioned her concerning the name of the shade—"was it what they called mauve or pale violet?"—and the material, "why Llama? when probably there was none of the wool of the genuine animal in it?"—and altogether succeeded in dashing her own pleasure in the dress. He talked in this way, not because his heart or even his taste was interested in the subject, but because he desired to make his own man and the waiters believe that the merest details connected with his young wife were of importance to him.

The morning hours slipped by. It was just on the point of striking eleven, and eleven was the hour at which she had requested Arthur Scorrier to come and see her. She rose up from the breakfast-table and went away into the adjoining room, and then stood at the window to watch the passers by and wait for Mr. Scorrier. Presently she saw him, not coming in, as in duty bound, to see what she had required of him, but going out with the two Misses Var-grave. At the same moment she felt her face flushing with a dark, angry red, and heard a footstep by her side. And she turned away, avowing to herself that she "was hunted and watched," as her husband said—

"What are you looking at, my dear?"

"The sea, I suppose," she said; "that is what every one comes to look at, or, at any rate, what every one says he or she comes to look at; I am going out now, to walk by it."

"To join the Vargraves?" he asked, glancing after the two girls and their escort, anxiously, as he spoke.

"No, indeed; I had quite enough of them last night. I am going by myself."

It was almost uttered, the offer he felt inclined to make of accompanying her. Almost uttered, but not quite. He remembered that he might stumble upon Mrs. Scorrier, and he could not bring himself to do so yet. So he suffered Amelia to go out by herself. And as soon as she left the hotel, she altered her avowed design of walking by the sea, and set off rapidly towards Mrs. Scorrier's house.

Mrs. Scorrier was at home, alone; and she welcomed Mrs. Hepburn with a warmth that left no doubt as to the reality and truth of her words being sincere. It was a delightful variation on the rather monotonous air of her life, this friendly, unfettered intercourse with a young worldly woman. For, unsophisticated and unworldly as Mrs. Scorrier was herself, she had a quick perceptive faculty, and this enabled her now to judge Amelia far more justly and completely than Amelia judged her.

For a few moments after Amelia sat down in the shady, chintz-furnished room that was redolent of quiet, and dried lavender, and peace, she felt herself to be in a very false position. Instinctively, she understood that her visit would perplex Mrs. Scorrier, and she knew that when old ladies are perplexed about a motive, they are apt to try to worry it out, and arrive at a full comprehension of it. On the face of it there was something absurd in her having come here, and Mrs. Hepburn sighed at this reflection, for she was not a woman who often suffered herself to be hurried into the performance of an absurd act. She felt that when it came to be known that she had made such a visit, her husband would find fault, and be disagreeably displeased, and the Vargraves would marvel, and Mr. Scorrier would laugh. As this last possibility occurred to her, she determined to waste no more time in useless repentance over a false step—if this coming here was a false step. So she quelled the kindly fuss which Mrs. Scorrier was making about the hot walk she must have had, and the umbrella she had carried to shade herself, and the superior advantages the lounge-chair possessed over the couch. She quelled all these amiable attempts to make her feel petted, and prized, and valued highly, and spoke abruptly about the thing that was uppermost in her mind.

"I should have saved myself the hot walk, and waited quietly for you to come and see me to-day, as it was agreed you should do, only I belong to my husband later in the day—he likes to drive, and wishes me to go with him—so as I did not wish to miss you, I thought I would come here, and ask you to forgive me for being so early."

"Not a bit too early," the old lady said, heartily. "As to that, indeed, I call it late; but I suit my hours to Arthur now, and we had only just done breakfast when he went out, half an hour before you came."

"I saw him going out with Miss Vargrave," Amelia said, quietly; "that is why I came. I knew you would be alone."

Old Mrs. Scorrier's face had flushed a little at the mention of Miss Vargrave. Her voice was a little troubled now, as she said,—

"Miss Vargrave and you are old friends, I think I have understood."

"Well, no," Amelia replied, with a great air of being perfectly frank at the cost of pain to herself. "I have known—no, I can't say I have 'known'—her for four or five years; but I have been in the habit of seeing her often during that time. Few people do know Cissy Vargrave; she either likes to affect that there is a mystery about herself, or there is some little mystery concerning her. I think the less one has to do with people about whom something can come out the better, don't you?"

Mrs. Scorrier, with the memory of the secret

and the sorrow that had darkened her own life vividly before her, said "Yes," but said it falteringly.

"So that is one reason," Amelia went on glibly, "why I don't get her to Glene to stay with me; my own wish would be to invite her there, and do the best I could for her; you know what I mean by that, Mrs. Scorrier— every woman knows, of course—but I think of what the consequences might be, and I do shrink from any responsibility. Young men visit at a house, and are apt to estimate visitors by the house they are visiting in; you know what I mean."

"Yes, I do," Mrs. Scorrier replied, lured into a confidence on the instant; "and I think it wonderful, and admirable, that you should have such consideration and forethought at your age; I feel and speak as a mother. Young men will be foolish where a pretty face is concerned; no one knows that better than I do." And the old lady shook her head, and looked as though she had experienced a world of woe through her son's wrong-headedness with regard to pretty faces.

"And it is the worst form of folly of which they can be guilty," Amelia responded, sagaciously, as if maternal cares connected with young men already weighed heavily upon her; "the very worst form of folly, for its effects may weight and hamper them through life. I often think," she went on, with suave maliciousness, "that poor Cissy is badly off indeed; no man, whose position is not perfectly well secured, will dare to marry her, and no man whose position is perfectly well secured will care to marry her."

"I really wish Mr. Hepburn would speak to him about it," Mrs. Scorrier said, excitedly, pursuing her own train of thought rather than answering Mrs. Hepburn's words. "Mr. Hepburn has such influence over Arthur, that even now, it's my firm conviction, he would pause if Mr. Hepburn asked him to, though he won't listen to me."

"About what?" Mrs. Hepburn asked, innocently.

"Why, about this young lady—this Miss Vargrave. I am sure I talked and talked last night till a stone would have been moved. I pointed out things to him that young people don't think of; but no, he won't take my experience, and will go on his own way; and I have hoped such different things for him."

" Do you mean that he is going to marry Miss Vargrave ? " Amelia said, rising up, and feeling that she was very pale, and that she had better get home to her hotel as soon as possible.

" I mean that he will, if she will have him," the mother said, sadly; and then Mrs. Hepburn's tones trembled with rage which she could not master, and for which she could not account, as she said,—

" If she will ! a nameless girl and a pauper is not likely to prove unwilling; she is too much a woman of the world not to know that Mr. Scorrier is most exceptionally unexacting in his requirements in a wife." Then she shook hands, carelessly, with the one whom she had kindly condescended to make so much more doubtful and unhappy than there was any need for her to have been made, and went back to Mr. Hepburn' who was tired and cross, by reason of having maintained an uncomfortable attitude at the window, with a field-glass in his hand, ever since she had left him.

"You said you were going to walk by the sea — and I have been watching for you," he said, testily, as she came into his presence.

"I changed my mind, and went into the town," she said.

"Where?"

"To Mrs. Scorrier's; you expressed a disinclination to receive her here, therefore politeness commanded that I should go to her, after having made an appointment for her to come to me."

"Since when have old women had such an attraction for you," he said, sneeringly, and there was something disagreeable, not to say aggravating, in Mr. Hepburn's expression when he desired to express derision.

"Since I have known how hard a thing it is to live always alone with an old man," she answered, in great exasperation; and then she took herself away to her own bedroom, there to bemoan the non-fulfilment of all the futile hopes she had built upon this marriage.

Altogether, it may easily be conceived that Mr. Hepburn was not in a fitting frame of mind to give a favourable reading to a letter which was put into his hands about two hours after this conversation with his wife. The letter was from Mrs. Scorrier, and was as follows :—

"Nine, The Crescent, Penzance.

" My DEAR SIR,—It is hard to address you directly, after so many years of indirect communication with, and checked interest in you. My excuse for breaking the bonds which have been imposed upon me,—'how' I know not, 'why,' I feel painfully,—is that I am bound to pursue any course that may possibly prove beneficial to my son, however unpleasant that course may be to me, and however greatly you may censure me for adopting it. You have always shown that you have Arthur's interest at heart —for his father's sake *only*, of that I am well aware. You have, also, always had great influence over him; he relies upon and respects you, and your judgment would have great weight with him in a matter where mine is entirely disregarded; this matter is his marriage. The young lady to whom he has offered his hand,

and who has won his heart, might satisfy the aspirations of a mother who had some better heritage to leave her son than I have to leave Arthur. As it is, I am in painful doubt that the shadow which is over her birth may but deepen the shadow which is over his; that shadow has clouded my life for more than thirty years. Is it any wonder that I would see all bright and clear about my son? We are strangers personally, but I feel assured that you will help me, for the sake of one we both loved. Get my boy to pause while there is yet time. Arthur will be sure to tell you of his affection for Miss Cecile Vargrave. I have talked the subject over with Mrs. Hepburn, who has just done me the honour to call upon me, and I cannot but wish that her conscientious views about it were shared by Mr. and Mrs. Vargrave. They are injudicious, not to say very wrong, in presenting this young lady, who is, I acknowledge, both beautiful and charming, under false colours to the world. If we could meet, I could point out, more forcibly than I can in writing, why such a marriage would be fatal to Arthur. Therefore, I ask you to see me—to cease to treat me as if

I had been the foe of your friend. Believe me to be,

> "My dear Sir,
> "Yours obediently,
> "Mabel Scorrier."

Mr. Hepburn's hand shook as he read through this appeal. When he came to the signature he read it aloud, and his wife, who had come back to the room, fancied that there was a tremor in his voice.

" Did you speak ? " she asked, indifferently.

"Eh! no ; that is, here is a letter which I wish you would answer for me," he answered, tossing it over to her little table. "Mrs. Scorrier writes to ask me to see her about some woman's folly that she has already discussed with you, I find."

She took the letter up and read it quickly ; then she said,—

" I will answer it, if you tell me what I am to say. You will see her ?—when shall it be ? "

" I will not see her," he said, raising his voice ; " I will not be persecuted, when I come

out for my health, by any folly of this sort.
Say to her—oh, say that I consider her son
to be quite capable of managing his own affairs
without any interference from me or from any-
one else; say what you like, in fact, only give
her to understand that I won't be harassed
about the matter, and that if I offer any counsel
to Arthur, it will be to the effect that he acts
as he deems best for himself."

" That will be rather a rude letter to write
to a mother who has paid you the compliment
of asking your advice about her son," Amelia
said, rising up and going to a writing-table;
" still, I am quite ready to write it; it does
not concern me ; I suppose the more concise I
make it the better ?"

" Decidedly," he said, curtly, and then she
proceeded to write as follows :—

" Mr. Hepburn presents his compliments to
Mrs. Scorrier, and, in answer to her two requests, begs to assure her that he sees no
reason for an interview with her, and no impediment to her son's marriage with Miss
Cecile Vargrave. Under this view of the

case, therefore, Mr. Hepburn begs to decline the honourable offices of counsellor and adviser.

"Queen's Hotel, Penzance."

"What have you said, my dear?" said Mr. Hepburn, as he saw his wife lay down her pen and pick up an envelope.

"Shall I read it to you?" she replied, feeling tolerably sure that in his haste to have done with the business, he would not accept her offer.

"Can't you tell me concisely what you have said?" he answered.

"I have said just what you told me to say," she said, folding up the note, sealing and addressing it as she spoke. "I have told her (with great civility, of course), that you must decline the honour she offers you; 'thrusts upon you' I might have said if I had not been polite; and that you think there is no impediment to Mr. Scorrier's marriage with Miss Vargrave; that's all you wanted said, isn't it?"

"Yes," he said, with a sigh of relief, "and I hope she will take it as a definite answer."

"Not but that I think it perfectly reasonable on her part, stupid old woman as she is, that she should object to such a marriage for her son; all respectable people have a prejudice in favour of legitimacy," Amelia said, scornfully; and then she thought of the thousand and odd ways in which it would be within the compass of her ability to make Mr. Scorrier regret the rashness of the step he was about to take.

"Cissy Vargrave will never smart under slights without making a sign," she thought, "and if she smarts, her husband will suffer for it."

Then, unfortunately for her own peace of mind, she placed herself at the window just in time to see Mr. Scorrier drive away from the hotel with the Vargraves. "He has been with them all day, and they would never allow that if it were not settled," she said to herself. It seemed to her now, that she might just as well go back to Glene, and establish herself in the neighbourhood as well as might be, before the bride came home. For that Cissy would soon be in Danebury as a bride she could not doubt.

Meantime, Mrs. Scorrier received and read the reply to her appeal to Mr. Hepburn; read it with tears in her eyes—tears which she was careful to wipe away before Arthur came home. " He is very unforgiving," she thought, " but he must have been a good man all his days, and I am only thankful that my Arthur should have such a friend."

END OF VOL. I.

J. Ogden and Co., Printers, 172, St. John Street, E.C.